UNDER WATER

A STRONG CURRENT TRILOGY BOOK 1

UNDER WATER

A STRONG CURRENT TRILOGY BOOK 1

GREG OLMSTED

Library of Congress Control Number: 2015905323

ISBN 978-0-9861089-0-7 (trade paperback)

FIRST EDITION

Printed in The United States of America

Book design by Gwyn Kennedy Snider

*"Every man is more than just himself; he also represents
the unique, the very special and always significant and
remarkable point at which the world's phenomena intersect,
only once in this way, and never again."*
HERMANN HESSE

CHAPTER ONE

THE DIVE INSTRUCTOR SURFACED, startling three ducklings. Frightened, they paddled across the dark water to the far side of the quarry, to the distant shore where the water's edge met dark-red sandstone. Liko watched as they scurried out and struggled up a steep bank and waddled along an eroded terrace. The ducklings looked funny; they were burnt orange. Liko wondered if last night's violent thunderstorm had washed red earth into the quarry, turning the water a rusty-red and dyeing the ducklings.

Liko cautiously leaned his 305 pounds against the wood railing of the old dock and then shifted his attention to the divemaster, his instructor, who was treading water.

"Six-inch visibility!" the divemaster cried, his mouth just above the water. "I need a flashlight. Who has a flashlight?"

You've got to be nuts, Liko thought. Trembling, he sat down on the gray, weathered planks and tucked his large hands deep into the front pocket of his gray hoodie. He looked into the bright sun and closed his eyes. He shivered.

He thought it strange that the sun was so bright but the air was so cold and the water so dark.

Splashing his way out of the water, the divemaster clambered onto the gray dock and stripped off his black rubber gloves and tank. "See if the caretaker has a flashlight," he ordered.

A female student stood up, eager to please.

Liko saw that her black wetsuit stretched tightly across her chest, flattening her breasts. The wetsuit hugged her narrow hips, too, giving her the appearance of a tomboy. Liko liked that. He watched as she obediently hurried towards the caretaker's trailer, crossing frost-covered, weathered sandstone, picking her way quickly across the cold and gritty earth, barefoot.

She soon returned with an underwater flashlight, small and blue with a short lanyard. Now standing next to the divemaster, she was standing between Liko and the sun, and her shadow settled on Liko. And then a triangle of blue sunlight flashed between her thighs. Liko stared. As she vigorously rubbed her hands together and shifted from foot to foot, the brilliant sunlight flashed—blue, platinum, blue.

Is she cold? Liko wondered. *Or is she nervous, like me?*

The divemaster shook the plastic flashlight, clicked it on and off, slammed it against the palm of his hand.

When the girl sat down on a green Coleman cooler next to her dive equipment piled on the dock, Liko found himself staring into the brilliant sun, so he closed his eyes. And again he shivered.

He was dead tired. He had slept two, maybe three hours last night.

Last night... his mother drank Bacardi rum and Coke, and then she passed out on her big sofa, leaving a pot of black-eyed peas simmering on the old electric stove.

Last night... he returned home from the late shift at the steak house and saw smoke billowing out the small kitchen window of their run-down trailer. He leaped up the metal steps and banged on the rusted screen door, yelling, "Mom! Mom! Open up!" But she didn't answer.

Overwrought, he tore the screen door from its worn-out hinges, but the front door was locked.

He pulled his pant pockets inside-out, but no keys. Where were they? In the trailer? In his bedroom? On his dresser?

"Help!" He rammed his large body against the door, but it was a solid metal door in a solid metal doorframe. A door intended to stop his abusive father.

Liko lost his balance and stumbled backwards down the steps, landing on his backside. Stunned, he picked himself up and stared at the old trailer in disbelief.

Smoke billowed out the small, high window. He considered climbing through it, but he was much too large.

"Help! Help!" He ran to a neighbor's trailer, but the neighbor wouldn't answer, wouldn't even turn on his porch light.

So he ran back, charged up the metal steps, and rammed the door again. It buckled but the metal frame held.

Finally a Las Vegas police cruiser roared down the street with blue lights flashing and sirens wailing. A half-minute later a police officer forced the front door with a crowbar. His partner entered, crouching low, keeping his head just below the layer of smoke. They found Liko's inebriated mother sprawled on her big brown sofa in front of a blaring Sony.

Everyone in the trailer park watched from across the street as the officers escorted her wobbling bulk—she was 6-feet tall, big-boned, obese—out of the trailer. They left her quavering on the sidewalk, frightened, coughing, and gasping for air.

Her fisted hands tugged at her purple tent of a nightgown and she collapsed onto cold concrete. Liko rushed to her side. She reached up and grabbed his hand and rested her head against his wide thigh, her downturned mouth heavy above a triple chin. Nervously, he stroked her thick black hair which, in the cold wind, wrapped around his large legs like sheet lava flowing around tree trunks.

An officer carried out the pot of burning beans and set it down on the sidewalk next to Liko's mother. Smoke rolled out of the blackened pot, enveloping her. Liko looked down into her face and saw irritated, bloodshot eyes.

A fire engine arrived.

Liko listened as the police explained to the firefighters that the emergency was just a pot of burning beans. He watched as the police officer pointed out his mother, as the firefighters shook their heads and the neighbors gawked.

He wanted to disappear.

Everyone left—the police, the firefighters, the smirking neighbors—and Liko and his mother returned to their trailer.

He shoved a large potted geranium against the ruined front door to keep it closed—the withered geranium a collection of dead sticks, lifeless branches, dried-up leaves.

Then his mother guzzled a few more Bacardi rum and Cokes. "To settle my nerves," she mumbled.

A short while later she was dancing a drunken hula, her big-boned hips sweeping to the left and then to the right, sending a chair and then a lamp smashing against the walls of the small trailer. She cried and sang "Sweet Leilani."

Liko sat alone in his tiny room, listening to their chrome and vinyl dinette set smash against the walls, listening to his mother's melancholy voice: "Sweet Leilani, heavenly flower oh, my lovely Leilani."

Late in the morning, about 3am, she passed out on her big tired sofa in front of the blaring television.

After that, Liko pulled an old Hawaiian quilt out of their battered suitcase, which she kept under her bed. He spread the once-colorful quilt, with its faded red hibiscus motif, over her large body. He gently kissed the deep furrows running across her forehead.

He loved her, but hated the Koholua genes they shared. Not only had he inherited her height—he was 6 feet 3 inches tall—but he had also inherited her big bones and her big body.

He turned off the television and retired to his bedroom.

Remembering his keys, he found them on top of his dresser and shoved them into his pants pocket. Now exhausted, he sat on the edge of his twin bed and stared at the small rectangular window high on the wall in his tiny room.

Liko's eyes sprang open. *What*? He shook his head and found himself sitting on the narrow, rotten, spongy dock. His mind jumped back to the present. Ten feet away, a heavy dive tank lay on its side on weathered gray planks. A student had bumped it, knocking it over.

Liko noticed that the other students had already changed into their wetsuits and were now checking their gear, so he hurriedly yanked off his sneakers, jumped up and stepped out of his cotton sweatpants, and pulled off his warm hoodie. Soon he was naked except for baggy blue swim trunks. Goosebumps rose on his brown skin.

He glanced at the girl sitting on the green cooler. Was she watching him, surveying his soft, undeveloped, undisciplined body? Embarrassed, he forced his feet through the narrow pant legs of his black wetsuit and gathered the neoprene around his calves. He smelled urine.

He stood up and tugged the soiled pants over his chubby knees, his bulky thighs, and up his size 46 waist, all the time trying not to breathe the ureic vapors. Aghast, he discovered his large stomach hanging over the tight waistband, like a large blob of toothpaste popping out the top of a tube squeezed hard from the bottom. Embarrassed, he cursed his Koholua genes.

He bent over slightly and stuck his finger into a small hole in a worn kneepad and wiggled it side-to-side. He turned the mask and snorkel over in his hand, noting that the plastic skirting and plastic tube were a dingy orange. He saw deep gouges on the sides of the metal air tank; he ran his finger down a particularly deep and wide one.

Liko stepped into the leg opening of the wetsuit top and pulled it up to his crotch. He then worked his arms backward into the heavy sleeves. When he straightened, the top stretched, conforming to his large frame. Then he sucked in his putai-like stomach and, holding his breath, zipped up the top, starting from his left hip, crossing his chest, and ending at his right shoulder.

I'm shrink-wrapped in black neoprene, he thought.

He spread his weight belt on the ground and stepped over it. After squatting to grab it, he stood up and hoisted it to the middle of his back. He bent forward and thirty-six pounds of dull gray lead settled onto the small of his back. He buckled the belt, straightened up, and his hips caught the deadweight. It felt as if he had tied a car battery to his waist.

He was puffing, exhaling short bursts of white vapor. Breathing was difficult. He unzipped the neoprene top halfway.

Then the girl walked over.

"Can I help?"

He nodded, yes, shyly.

She lifted his buoyancy control jacket and tank, groaning, her arms shaking, her body straining. Yet she held it—the jacket and heavy tank—up in the air for him.

Speechless, he turned his back to her and slid his arms into the jacket as if he was putting on a bulky winter coat. She held it up against his back as he adjusted the shoulder straps and fastened the jacket's belt.

"Thanks," he said softly with a diffident smile.

She then kneeled to ready his dive boots.

He grabbed the rotten wood railing and raised a foot. She held the bootie steady as he wiggled his 14-inch, EEE foot into the stretching material. The zipper on the side of the bootie wouldn't close, but she was able to fasten the Velcro strap.

As she helped him with the second bootie, he could smell the shampoo in her hair: a bouquet of flowers.

She stood and handed him the bib hood. He pulled it securely over his head, tucking the flanged bottom under the neck of the jacket.

"Just like an underwater warrior."

"What?" The hood covered his ears. "What did you say?"

"The designer stripe."

"The what?"

"The red stripe!" she said, raising her voice. She leaned forward and her fingers darted to his forehead and then slid along the red stripe, following it over the smooth crest of the black neoprene hood to the base of his wide neck.

"What?" he repeated.

"It looks like a red Mohawk!"

He felt his heart pounding because the hood was pressing against the carotid artery in his neck, reducing the flow of blood to his brain. He felt dizzy.

Then she helped him put on the adjustable fins—the ones with the quick-release mechanism—and the dingy orange mask and snorkel.

And then, as quickly as she had come over to help, she left and returned to her spot on the gray dock, and sat down on the green cooler, and began studying her dive manual.

Alone again, Liko felt ashamed and claustrophobic. The wetsuit was too small and there was that urine smell; the weight belt and old tank were dangerously heavy; the tight hood made him dizzy. And had she made some crack about him looking like a Mohawk?

Was it time to don the wetsuit gloves? He looked them over: gray palms, a thumb and—they were mittens!

How can I—

But then the divemaster called out, "Everybody ready?"

"Ready?" Liko replied sarcastically. "Like a damned walrus!"

Everyone laughed.

Liko had not meant his reply as a joke, and he didn't like being laughed at.

He took a deep breath and avoided eye contact with the students. Instead, he gazed at the still surface of the flooded quarry. Where were the ducklings?

His eyes searched for the rusty-orange puffs and soon he found them. They were still on the far shore, waddling on the red, eroded bank, still hunting for insects in deep furrows where the iron-stained earth had washed away into the quarry.

He watched as a lone duckling waddled to the edge of the eroded terrace. He saw it slide on the clay-rich weathered sandstone and tumble into the dark water.

"Let's go!" the divemaster ordered.

Liko clamped his mouth around the rubber mouthpiece of the regulator and took a shallow breath of supplied air. It tasted metallic, and the air dragged through the supply hose like a Wendy's Frosty sucked through a straw.

With the side of his mittened hand, he clumsily pushed the low-pressure inflation valve on his jacket. The jacket instantly inflated in all directions, including inward. The tight squeeze startled him. He released some air from the jacket and that lessened the squeeze. But he still felt claustrophobic: the wetsuit, the bib hood, the booties, and even the gloves—all were tight, too tight.

He looked out over the rusty water. *This sure ain't the YMCA pool.*

It's an underwater junkyard, that's what the divemaster had told them when the students first arrived, when they took their places along the length of the dock. He had warned them, "Everything you can imagine is down there: a burnt-up Ford Pinto; a rusted-out van lying on its side, leaching toxic metals from psychedelic painted flowers; a Harley Davidson; even the fuselage of a crop duster that crashed in a cornfield near here, killing the pilot." Fire. Rust. Toxins. Vanity. Pesticides. Blood.

Slowly, Liko's thoughts rose from the depths of the quarry and his gaze swept the surface of the dark water. Where was the duckling that had tumbled from the ledge?

Had something pulled it under? A large catfish?

He spotted three turtles—one large and two small—sunning on gnarled deadwood that was partially submerged. He noted a dark vermiculate pattern and a hint of yellow on the two smaller turtles. But it was the large turtle he would remember because, although it was drab and without marbling, the sun glinted off its wet shell.

"Jump on in," the divemaster ordered Liko. "It's not getting any warmer."

Liko glanced furtively over at the girl. Still sitting on the cooler she looked up from her dive manual. They made eye contact.

Her eyes are worried, he thought.

He looked out over the surface of the water. It looked dull, dark, rusty. Still. *Too still.*

Gripping the weight belt firmly with both hands, Liko took a giant stride off the dock and, for a brief moment, he felt suspended in air. Then he plunged through the glassy surface like a ledge of sandstone falling off the surrounding wall. Whomp! The sudden impact with the cold water ripped the mask off his face. Instinctively he grabbed it and closed his eyes.

Ten feet? Fifteen feet? Gradually, his descent stopped. And then the air in his jacket launched him back to the surface, where he bobbed up and down like a tuna float.

He blinked his eyes, cautiously, focusing on the distant shore and the three turtles. He could see that the large turtle was still wet—at least his contacts had not washed out.

Then he retrieved the mouthpiece, which had been knocked out of his mouth. He popped it back in and tested it; it still worked, and the air still tasted metallic.

He donned his facemask after pouring out the water. The strap tangled in his wavy black hair but he ignored it. The dingy Plexiglas instantly fogged up and obstructed his vision.

He now noticed that cold water had flowed into his wetsuit, between his skin and the heavy layer of neoprene foam—much colder than he had expected. Shivering, he relaxed his bladder and warm urine filled the suit. The warmth felt good.

Awkwardly, he dogpaddled to the divemaster and the buoy in the center of the flooded quarry, dragging his over-inflated jacket, his heavy air tank, and his big body through the water. All the while he was drawing down the air in his tank, breathing hard.

I have to do this, he told himself. *I have to get certified.*

When he arrived at the buoy the divemaster handed him a four-pound weight. "To compensate for the buoyancy of your wetsuit."

Bullshit, Liko thought, as he squeezed the fist-sized lead weight into the utility pocket of his jacket. He now carried thirty-eight pounds of deadweight plus the heavy metal tank.

Holding on to the buoy, he listened to the divemaster, a last-minute substitute, a man he had met just this morning. In a gruff voice the divemaster explained that they would descend to an underwater wooden platform. He explained that the platform was held under the surface by ropes anchored to the bottom of the quarry. The ropes kept the platform from launching to the surface. He said that the buoy, which Liko was holding onto, was attached to the underwater platform by a descent line. Liko was to follow the descent line down to the platform. There he would wait for the divemaster to switch the flashlight on and off three times, signaling Liko to demonstrate his diving skills.

"First, take off your mask and then put it on again."

No problem. I'll keep my eyes shut.

"Then throw your regulator over your shoulder, find it before you run out of air, and pop it back into your mouth."

No problem. I can hold my breath.

"And the last thing I want you to do—float a few feet above the platform. Show me you've mastered buoyancy control."

Liko shivered. He had practiced neutral buoyancy control

in the indoor YMCA pool; however, instead of floating in a stationary position a few feet above the bottom of the pool, he had always popped to the surface.

I can do it. This time I WILL do it!

"If you screw up and rocket to the surface and blow out your lungs, then you don't pass. You understand?"

You're an asshole, Liko thought.

"Any questions?"

"How deep is—"

The divemaster interrupted, "Hold on to the rope, Mr. Walrus, as you go down. Remember, when you reach the bottom wait for my signal. I'll flash three times." He held the flashlight over his head and clicked it on and off three times. Then he slipped beneath the surface of the water.

Offended and miffed because the divemaster had cut off his question and called him "Mr. Walrus," Liko let air out of his jacket, exhaled, and began his descent. The slick nylon rope slid across the palm of his mitten.

At one body length below the surface he paused, gripping the rope in a vice-like hold, suspended in the murky water. With his free hand, he pinched his nose through the silicon skirting of his facemask, closed his mouth, and blew hard. His ears popped as air rushed into his Eustachian tube and sinus spaces, stabilizing his ears. Then he continued downward, following the slick rope.

When he caught up with the divemaster, another body-length down, the man gripped the front of Liko's jacket and waved the flashlight back and forth in front of Liko's face. In response Liko raised his hand directly in front of his mask and brought his thumb and mittened fingers together to form a circle, signaling "I'm okay," even though he still felt insulted.

Liko guessed that the visibility was six inches. *This is crazy,* he thought.

But then the divemaster again descended. Liko followed, reluctantly, sliding along the rope, also descending feet first.

And then total darkness. Zero light. What had happened? It was as if he had gotten out of bed in the middle of the night, switched on an overhead light for a brief moment, and then flicked it off again. Instant blindness. He was surrounded in all directions by cold, pitch-black water. Later he would learn that he had entered a layer of suspended red clay that blocked all sunlight.

And the rope was now slick like slimy rhubarb, sliding away when he tried to get a better grip. Liko slashed the darkness in front of him, but the rope had vanished. He slashed to his left, then to his right. No rope. Nothing.

His heart hammered in his chest and he felt his body suddenly grow hot. He took deeper breaths. He sucked harder on the mouthpiece. Each breath was like sucking air from a deflated carcass.

And then a surge of energy.

Panic? I must not panic!

Disoriented, he stared into malevolent emptiness, unsure which way was up, which way was down.

I'll ascend, he thought. He kicked hard with his fins and was soon moving swiftly through the darkness, yet aimlessly. He hoped that he was returning to the surface.

After a few tense moments, he broke through the silt layer

and saw the fuzzy light. Again, six-inch visibility. Relieved, he pumped his fins harder and surfaced.

He squinted in the bright sunlight.

He tore out his mouthpiece and breathed fresh, cold air deep into his lungs. The cold air burnt his lungs like iodine on an open wound.

Then his eyes darted to the dock thirty feet away where he thought the girl would be. Yes, she waved. He wanted to wave back but he was too embarrassed.

After a long time—*time enough to drown*, Liko thought—the divemaster surfaced. He swam over to Liko and in an agitated, loud voice exclaimed, "What happened?"

When Liko didn't immediately reply, he added, "What are you supposed to do when you get separated?"

Liko was afraid that his voice would crack, revealing how nervous he was, and the girl would hear—she would hear his voice crack. They were floating in the middle of the flooded quarry, but the rock walls magnified the dive instructor's voice. She would hear. Even his treading of water sounded to him like splashing.

The divemaster scolded him, "If you surface, you must let your buddy know."

Liko's reply was short and focused. "Right. Sorry." He heard the fear in his voice.

"If you get separated underwater, look for your buddy. If you can't find each other *then* you surface. Understand?"

Liko nodded, yes.

He could feel the girl watching him, but he didn't look in her direction again. He knew that she had heard the scolding.

"Are you ready to try it again?"

"Yes."

"Okay, this time I will follow *you* down." The divemaster paused, then added, "And remember, signal me if you decide to surface." Then he placed his hand on top of Liko's hand, which was holding onto the buoy.

Liko cringed. He wanted to yank his hand away. Instead, he gritted his teeth and moved his hand from the buoy to the rope.

The divemaster grabbed the rope too, and his heavy hand slid down and rested on top of Liko's hand again.

And then they descended.

This time, when Liko reached the silt layer he paused. He wanted to observe it, to contemplate it—the interface between light and dark—but he did not have the luxury of time.

Instead, he descended, passing through the penumbra. And again, it was as if a bright light had been flicked on and off, producing total darkness. But this time his gloved hand didn't slip, and he followed the rope all the way down to the platform where he planted his feet, precariously.

The divemaster joined him. His hand once again pinned Liko's hand to the rope.

Before Liko could get his bearings, the divemaster stuck the underwater flashlight against Liko's mask, directly on the glass lens plate. Then he flashed it on and off three times—directly into Liko's eyes.

What a jerk, Liko thought. Phantom bright lights, like the shiny eyes of sea creatures, appeared and stared at him.

He pulled his hand free from the divemaster's, wrapped

his elbow around the line, closed his eyes tightly to protect his soft contacts, and removed his mask.

He still saw the phantom lights, even with his eyes tightly shut.

He started to count to fifteen so the divemaster would have plenty of time to observe that he had taken off the mask. When he reached twelve seconds he realized that the divemaster couldn't see much, if anything. It wasn't a powerful flashlight.

After that he donned the mask, pressing the plastic skirt firmly against his face and pulling the strap over his head. He tried to check for hair caught between the skirt and his forehead, but his fingers were useless inside the mittens.

He tipped the bottom of the mask off his face, tilted his head back and, hoping the top of the mask would make a tight seal even if some hair was trapped beneath the skirt, he gently blew air through his nose and into the mask. He felt the water drain from the bottom of the mask as it filled with air.

Will the seal hold?

Cautiously, he opened his eyes. It was still pitch dark so he couldn't tell if his contacts were okay. The phantom lights had disappeared, though.

He waited—patiently waited—until the divemaster shone the flashlight in his eyes again. This time there were three weak flashes of light. No phantom lights.

Are the batteries dying?

Determined to demonstrate his mastery of buoyancy control, Liko let go of the rope and dropped to his knees on the platform. He then stretched out flat on his stomach against the wooden planks. It was time to perform the neutral buoyancy fin pivot.

He added small spurts of air to his jacket. Nothing happened. He added another spurt.

Growing impatient, he held down the inflation button a little longer. Still no change. Again, a little longer.

He began to rise. He added more air. But then he was rising too fast, so he grabbed for the wooden planks. His mittened hands slipped between the planks. Wedged tight.

Anchored there, he considered his predicament. If he let go he would have a runaway ascent. On the other hand, if he held on no one would know; after all, the divemaster couldn't see. So why let go? To earn his certification, to escape from the trailer park, to get away from his mom, to get a ticket to Hawaii—those were his goals. The skill wasn't important. To escape was everything.

Thus he made his decision. He freed one hand and stripped all the air from his jacket. Immediately he sank onto the platform. He aligned his body along the floor, the tips of his fins and his stomach resting against the wood, his nose an inch from a plank. Again he wedged his free hand between the planks. He executed ten perfect pushups. After that he freed both hands, returned to his knees, and sat upright.

One or two minutes passed, which gave him an opportunity to think.

God, it's dark!

How big is this platform?

Where are the wrecked cars? The mangled motorcycles? The crashed planes?

But then something bumped him. And then something struck his head. He flinched. But then he realized that it was the divemaster, come to test him on his last skill. So he waited patiently while the divemaster's gloved hands groped their way up Liko's chest to his mask. He waited for the three flashes, but instead the divemaster tapped Liko's mask three times with the flashlight. *It's dead*, Liko thought.

He had one skill left to perform: he had to remove the air supply from his mouth, throw the regulator over his right shoulder, and then recover it using an extended arm-sweep. Until he recovered the mouthpiece, he would be without air.

For a brief moment he considered whether or not to try it. After all, the divemaster couldn't see him. Yet Liko thought that it wasn't a difficult skill to perform; the mouthpiece was connected to a hose that was connected to the tank, so it was impossible to completely lose the mouthpiece. Why not try it? *Besides*, he told himself, *I can do it.*

So in one smooth motion he removed the mouthpiece and threw it over his shoulder. Then he counted fifteen full seconds.

From his upright position, he lowered his right shoulder and extended his right arm to his side and reached to recover the mouthpiece. He came up empty-handed.

He forced himself to focus.

He leaned backwards, fully extending his right arm behind himself, felt the bottom of his tank, and then swept his arm forward. Again he came up empty-handed.

He felt a twinge in his stomach.

He remembered the reach method: the regulator was attached to a hose attached to the air tank. All he had to do was find the place where the air-supply hose attached to the air tank and follow the air supply hose to its end—and there would be the regulator, the mouthpiece, and his air.

Quickly, he reached behind his head to the base of his neck. His gloved hand felt something solid—the top of the tank?

Damned gloves!

His mittened hand enclosed a hose and he followed it ... to an oval console. The oval shape told him that it was the pressure and depth gauge.

Wrong hose!

His lungs began to ache.

He tried to tear the gloves off but he couldn't grasp the Velcro straps wrapped around his wrists.

He felt his body trembling. He started to panic.

He forced himself to pause, to stop, to do nothing, to focus, to reorient himself in space and time. That was a skill he had learned long ago, to protect himself from his father on a drunk. Yes, he could become quiet and disappear in time and space. So now he focused.

He reached behind with his left hand, found the bottom of the tank, and raised it up along his back. With his right hand he reached behind his head and grabbed all the hoses. He thought he felt two hoses, but he was uncertain.

Damned gloves!

He leaned forward, resting the tank on his back. Then he freed his left hand and separated the hoses. Yes, there were two. He took a hose in his right hand and a hose in his left. He followed them to their ends. There was the depth gauge. And there was the mouthpiece! And his air! He popped it in.

It was then that he realized that he was forward somersaulting—over and over and over again.

He tried to blow the water out of the mouthpiece, but his lungs were empty. He knew that he had to purge the mouthpiece, otherwise his first gulp of air would mix with water and he would inhale the water deep into his lungs, and then he would panic and drown.

And then he remembered: *A purge button . . . on the mouthpiece. If I push it and inhale, push it and inhale, at the same time....*

Air filled his lungs.

And then his tank struck something solid. He heard a muted, underwater sound—metal striking rock. The impact shook his body. His limbs seemed weightless.

Am I resting on the bottom of the quarry with my tank underneath me and my feet and arms dangling above me? Or did I bounce off something? Am I still falling?

He felt behind him, felt something solid. *Damned gloves!* He decided it was the floor of the quarry.

At least I recovered the regulator! It wasn't graceful, but I recovered it. I've earned my certification! And if the divemaster is searching for me, fine. Let him search. I can wait a minute or two. But I'm not searching. Not down here— it's too dangerous.

He forced himself to breath slowly.

He recalled the brief feeling of weightlessness as he was falling. He wondered if that was how the astronauts felt as they floated in dark, empty space.

As he relaxed, he began to shiver. He knew that the cold water conducted his body heat away 20 times faster than air did. He recalled that fact from a training lecture at the YMCA.

He held the depth gauge on the console up to his facemask but couldn't see anything, even though it was supposed to fluoresce in the dark. He tried to equalize his ears, but the pressure difference was now too great between the air in his ear passages and the pressure of the water at the bottom of the quarry. He should have equalized his ear passages in stages as he descended. Now it was too late and his ears ached—it was a steady, squeezing pressure.

How deep did I fall?

Liko waited several minutes, but as he expected, the divemaster didn't find him. Deciding to surface, he inflated his jacket and shot upwards. A runaway ascent!

Something swooshed by, suddenly—black and large, directly in front of him. It passed within inches of his nose. And then he realized, too late: *The wooden platform! I could have broken my neck!*

He rocketed through the silt layer and into the zone of six-inch visibility, and then a moment later he shattered the surface of the dark water. He spit out the mouthpiece.

Fortunately, during his runaway ascent he had unconsciously exhaled, which had prevented his lungs from expanding and bursting. And now, floating in his inflated jacket, he whirled counter-clockwise, looking for the divemaster. He didn't see him.

The sun hurt his eyes.

He dogpaddled to the yellow buoy and held tightly onto it.

That was insane, he thought, as his body flooded with

endorphins. *That was the most reckless thing I've done in my life.* He felt short of breath. *Wow! Better than the Manhattan Express!*

The Manhattan Express was a roller coaster in the New York-New York Hotel and Casino at the south end of the Strip where Tropicana Avenue intersected Las Vegas Boulevard. It was a 67mph ride with two inversions and a 144-foot drop. Liko loved that ride as a kid.

After a few moments the divemaster surfaced.

Before he could say anything, Liko explained: "I fell off the platform." The sound of his voice surprised him: his voice was deeper. "Hey, how deep is the quarry?"

The divemaster said, "It's 175 feet deep," and nothing else.

Liko dogpaddled his over-inflated jacket, his air tank, and his large body awkwardly back to the dock.

I should learn how to swim.

Reaching the boat dock, he smiled up at the girl. *Don't let go the rope!* he wanted to tell her, but he was too shy to speak up.

The girl drowned.

CHAPTER TWO

LIKO SAT IN THE EMERGENCY EXIT SEAT, transfixed, staring out the oval window into the early afternoon sunlight. This was his first flight, at least that he could remember. He had flown once before as an infant, but in the opposite direction, from Hawaii to Nevada.

He shivered and rubbed his forearms for warmth and covered his massive upper body with one of the thin navy blue courtesy blankets. He stretched out his long legs in the extra space provided in the emergency exit row. Almost comfortable, he rested his temple against the cool plastic that framed the thick glass of the oval window.

He thought about his mother. Standing in her big faded pink *muumuu*, the one with the black hibiscus print, she'd cried when they'd said goodbye. He'd glanced over his shoulder as he had boarded the bus to the airport and saw her watching, her hands at her large dark eyes, wiping away the tears. She'd looked so helpless surrounded by strangers.

He placed a small white pillow between his head and the window and closed his eyes. Liko tried to forget about his mother and tried, instead, to imagine what lay ahead in Hawaii. But his mind wandered.

He daydreamed about a cuddly young girl with gentle hands, a girl who wanted to share her body with him. And then he imagined that she was a tomboy, a quixotic co-adventurer with a mischievous smile, a girl to travel the world with. And as they traveled she became a young woman and his ladyfriend, his steady companion, clearheaded, someone who understood him. And then the daydream ended.

Longing for her and hoping that she was not air-built like the white clouds below him, he sighed. Maybe he would meet her in Hawaii?

Again he sighed. Hawaii.... He had asked his uncle for an invitation to Hawaii every year since the fifth grade. At the beginning of each school year, he wrote his uncle asking permission to visit during summer vacation. In reply, each year—for five years—he received a Christmas card from Waikiki, but the answer was always the same: "When you are older."

"Your uncle works," his mother explained. "He can't take care of you during the day. Maybe when you are older."

But then last winter, during the middle of his sophomore year, his uncle sent a card with a Santa making a snow angel in the sand: "Ho! Ho! Ho! Liko, learn to scuba dive and you can come for the summer. Mele Kalikimaka. Your uncle, Keahi."

Liko was ecstatic; his mother, distressed. He argued that it would be a great adventure. She argued that he was too young. "You're only seventeen. Only a sophomore."

"I can take care of myself, you know I can."

Her dark eyes assessed him. "You don't know your uncle." His mother paused, shook her head. "Spending a summer with your uncle...."

"What?" he complained. "What about uncle?"

She pursed her lips, shook her head, again. "Uncle K had a beautiful voice. He was the best chanter at the Ho'olaulea Festival for two years in a row. Two times he won. No one had a more beautiful voice. His voice was a gift."

"So," he shrugged, "so he sings?"

His mother chuckled at that. "No, Liko, you no understand. Your uncle had a *gift*. He could have been a great chanter, a great hula dancer, a great teacher. In the days of King Kamehameha—in the days of the great Hawaiian monarchy—he would have been *kahuna nui*." She paused, frowned, "You no understand?"

Liko shook his head, no.

"A *kahuna* is a priest. Your uncle could have been *kahuna nui*, high priest. He could have started his own *halau*. He could have been *kumu hula*. Instead...." She sighed and then added, "And now life pass him by, like me." Her face was screwed into a scowl. "No, Liko."

"Why not?"

"Because . . . because my brother likes men."

"Really?" Liko thought about that. It seemed irrelevant. "No worry, Mom. I'm six foot three, 300 pounds."

His mother's caustic laugh boomed out and the rolls of

flesh around her middle shook. "You big? You're a puppy. Uncle K is twice as big. Even I am bigger than you."

Liko frowned. *We're monsters*, he thought. *I hate our genes.*

But then, seeing his disappointment, she said, "Let me think about it."

And she did think about it; she spent the next four days drinking rum and Cokes from the comfort of her trailer, and taking slow, unsteady walks around the trailer park. Liko watched the neighbors peeking out their small, high windows, their faces partially hidden by plastic curtains. He despised his neighbors and he loathed the trailer park.

Finally, on the morning of the fifth day, his mother told him to invite the neighbors to a *luau*. He reluctantly obeyed. He gritted his teeth; he knocked on their doors; he invited them.

Fortunately, it was a small trailer park and only a few were interested. Several eyed him suspiciously. One trailer was filled with love birds and shrouded in bird shit. The young woman who lived there fed the sparrows and pigeons and thousands of other birds that roosted in the branches of the myrtle that overhung her trailer. He didn't knock on her door because there was bird shit on the front steps and birdshit covered the black metal hand railing, too. It was even on the sidewalk. So instead of knocking, he yelled an invitation from the sidewalk. She yelled back angrily through a screened but birdshit-smeared door, "Don't scare my birds! I'll call the police!"

And he didn't knock on the door of the trailer with the three buffed Harleys parked in the dirt yard, either—for obvious reasons.

Early afternoon, he watched his mother cook a feast: a large juicy ham, thick yellow cornbread, yams with melted marshmallows—all his favorites. He reveled in the smells, marveling at how such a great feast could be prepared in such a small kitchen.

Late afternoon, he gathered four picnic tables and placed them in a semi-circle in the middle of the street, directly in front of his mother's trailer. Then he placed abandoned tires across the street on both sides to keep out cars. Since they lived on a loop, he thought no one would mind.

A couple of kids rode up on their skateboards, bouncing off the curb.

"You stunt junkies, get!"

One tucked his board under his arm, while the other attempted a half-hearted handstand. They went a short distance down the loop and then started riding again, smacking their boards, chipping the curbs.

At dusk, after he set out all the food on the picnic tables and all the guests were seated, Liko met his mother at the front door of their trailer. She was wearing the faded pink *muumuu* with the black hibiscus print.

He took her arm and escorted her through the doorway, down the iron steps and cold sidewalk, to the street. Arm-in-arm he guided her around the semi-circle of picnic tables and guests. She walked gracefully. A few neighbors acknowledged her as she passed. And then she took her seat at the head of the *luau*, next to her boombox and a case of red wine.

Liko surveyed the motley guests. All in all, there was no one that he wanted to see again after the luau, definitely, no one he would miss. Tonight he would keep their glasses filled with cheap wine. Tomorrow he would escape.

In the meantime he watched them devour the food and guzzle the wine.

And his mother? Well, after *her* third glass, she proclaimed the good news: "Liko is returning to his birthplace, Hawaii." And then she proudly announced that he was full-blooded Hawaiian. She declared that he would now learn his Hawaiian roots—his history, the culture of his people.

She proclaimed the good news as if she expected that all the guests would return home to their trailers and call their friends and spread the news that the world had changed.

But sitting to the right of his mother and listening to her proclamation, Liko felt uncomfortable. Why did she have to announce that he was full-blooded Hawaiian? What was that all about? He was going to Hawaii for the girls, the beaches, the adventure, but most especially, to escape the trailer park and his mother. That had nothing to do with his ancestry. He had no interest in his Hawaiian roots and that kind of thing. *She's got it all wrong*, he thought to himself. *She doesn't have a clue.*

The day after the *luau* he had written to Uncle Keahi, who promptly replied with a short note: "Aloha! Great to hear the good news, Liko. As soon as you get scuba certified, let me know. Then I will send you a roundtrip ticket. I look forward to diving this summer!"

Scuba certified? Roundtrip ticket? Diving?

So Liko enrolled in a beginning scuba class, but he didn't tell his mother because she would have forbidden it. Why? Because he couldn't swim.

In April, after passing the class, Liko mailed Uncle Keahi a photocopy of his scuba diving card and Uncle K kept his promise and promptly mailed a roundtrip airline ticket. Liko was disappointed to receive an electronic ticket; there was no return ticket he could tear up.

Nevertheless, he made up his mind. His mother, their trailer, the neighbors: these were all reasons for never returning. He was tired of the humiliation. And the flooded quarry? A shiver crept along his spine as he remembered the girl who had drowned; why hadn't he told her to keep hold of the rope?

Now, months later, he opened his eyes and gazed out the window at the clouds and the Pacific Ocean. Everything was bright white and shades of blue. Summer had arrived.

Is Uncle Keahi really twice as big as me? Will he be waiting at the Honolulu airport wearing a gaudy, bright aloha shirt, size 3XL?

The plane descended and its shadow grew larger against the clouds, until the shadow looked like a black bird with a long, thick bill—a crow, maybe. Liko laughed to himself and wondered if there was such a thing as a Hawaiian crow.

His thoughts continued to jump from present to past.

He remembered what his mother had told him last week about his childhood. She said he was two weeks old when the three of them—she, Liko, and his father—had moved to Las Vegas from Hawaii.

She said gambling aggravated his father's drinking, and the combination made his father mean. Consequently, the frequent beatings.

During their first year in Las Vegas his father sold most of their belongings, and to pay off gambling debts, he even sold her precious Niihau shell necklace—a wedding gift from Great Auntie.

The drinking and gambling and beatings continued until one evening, when Liko was four years old, his mother gathered him up into her large arms and said to him in a whisper, "How's my little pup? How's my little pup with the big hands and the big feet." Quietly, she carried him out the back door as his father snored in a drunken stupor in front of the blaring television.

Battered and abused, she'd walked-out, leaving everything behind: clothes, photo albums, pots and pans. But she'd protected her pup. She'd walked away and started over again. That had taken courage, and that was the reason he still loved her.

Now, thirteen years had passed and Liko knew that the metal door on their trailer and the old suitcase under his mother's bed were his father's legacy to him. The metal door kept his father out, in case he showed up. And the old suitcase was always ready, so that Liko and his mom could quickly escape and not leave everything behind again, like they had the first time.

The shadow of the plane grew larger as the plane descended and flew closer to the clouds. Liko now saw the heavy body, broad wings and rounded tail of a hawk: a large bird of prey gliding over the white clouds. *To be a hawk*, he thought, *to soar with no history to hold me back.*

Suddenly the silhouette was surrounded by a bright halo of colored rings, as small droplets of water redirected sunlight back towards Liko and the sun. The hawk, now in the center of the halo, turned red.

Liko thought again about the girl who'd drowned a few weeks ago. He had seen them pull her body from the water. He had witnessed her dead body.

And I'm not responsible!

Stomach acid rose into his throat. It burned.

The plane descended into the foggy white clouds for a few seconds before breaking through into blue sky again, and then Liko got his first view of Oahu. He was startled to see tall buildings. The entire coastline was overdeveloped. *So this is what Mom calls 'the gathering place.'* He caught a glimpse of gridlocked traffic on a highway that snaked along the coast between the ocean and the mountains.

He remembered his mother's instruction to call his great-aunt. He was to visit her shortly after his arrival.

He remembered his great-aunt said funny things. He recalled a story his mother had told him. He had been four, maybe four-and-a-half years old. His great-aunt stood in the doorway of their trailer during a brief visit to Las Vegas. Liko had run up to her quickly and pinched her leg. to which she had exclaimed, "Auwe, he attacks like a *nene!*"

Liko had looked up at his mother, puzzled.

His mother had explained, "A *nene* is a goose. A special Hawaiian goose." She turned to his great-aunt and apologized, "He thinks he is protecting me."

Now, here he was soaring alongside Waikiki Beach in a Boeing 767. Now, when he thought of his great-aunt he felt embarrassed. She had visited their trailer shortly after they had fled from his father. She knew how they lived, and that his mother was an alcoholic. His great-aunt probably knew what happened to the necklace she'd given his mother, too. Consequently, Liko had no plans to see her.

Everything was an embarrassment.

His stomach lurched. The burning had risen to the back of his throat and was almost unbearable.

He tried to concentrate on other things, on what lay ahead. He wanted to forget about being a native Hawaiian. He was determined to leave all that behind him, to go out into the world, to discover himself, to fulfill his personal destiny. *Yes*, he said to himself, *that's what I want.*

He was taken aback, though, at how ugly, how uninviting it looked: tall buildings like upright corncobs wedged between the coast and mountains; gridlock traffic; houses smothering the mountainsides. How disappointing. He suspected that the people here spent their lives pursuing money and stuff, just like back home—working by day, exhausted by night, never enjoying their mountains or their ocean. Sadness swept over him.

I should have run away to San Diego. Or San Francisco. Or Sacramento.

He steeled himself to make the best of it. Besides, if things didn't work out, he'd just run away again.

In the meantime, the money was in the old suitcase, safely hidden in the lining, along with his most cherished possessions. His mother had insisted that he use their old suitcase. She had taken out the Hawaiian quilt and carefully wrapped it in a black garbage bag and then tucked it underneath her sagging bed. He had packed stuff that he didn't want to leave behind, all the while thinking about how the suitcase was serving its intended purpose – kind of.

Looking out the small window again, he focused on the mountains. They were green, inviting, a beautiful contrast to the strangled coastline.

He wondered what it would be like to hike along a ridge. He closed his eyes and saw it clearly, a knife-edged ridge with steep drop-offs. Below him were lush valleys. He imagined that he was on a narrow trail, climbing to the summit of a mist-shrouded mountain. He felt a steady wind on his face. He watched clouds form and blow into the valley. It rained and he saw the runoff fill small streams. He saw cascading waterfalls. He saw swollen streams churn through the valleys. He saw everything flow into the ocean. And there were no tall buildings. No urban runoff. It was paradise.

The plane landed smoothly and Liko collected his tan backpack from the overhead compartment and followed the other passengers down the aisle.

It was time to meet Uncle Keahi. *I bet he is a fat alcoholic like Mom and Dad. And the gay thing, no worry. As soon as I get my feet under me, I'm leaving him behind too. I can take care of myself. No one is going to push me around, pin me down, and climb on top of ME. Hell no!*

Liko entered the baggage area and he looked around for his uncle. He noticed a cute Asian girl in tight blue jeans placing a flower lei around the neck of a short, Caucasian man. Another Asian woman was holding a small sign over her head; the oriental characters were unfamiliar. She was pretty, maybe Chinese? Or perhaps she was Korean or

Filipino or Vietnamese or Taiwanese or . . . he had no idea.

He looked around and saw faces with similar features, yet somehow different. He smiled to himself. There was a whole world of girls here in Hawaii!

Then Liko noticed a tall, heavy set, darkly tanned man standing against the wall behind a tour group. He was dressed casually in a Gold's Gym T-shirt, navy blue shorts, and flip-flops. Screened on the chest of his T-shirt was a drawing of a weightlifter wearing a green ti lei and curling a barbell. The man saw Liko and started across the room towards him.

Good God! Must be a security guy. What does he want with me? But why is he dressed so casual?

Liko noticed that people noticed this man, too. It was not only his size—he was slightly taller than Liko, at least 6 feet 4 inches—but also his muscular build and his graceful, effortless walk. And his smile: perfect, white teeth.

An entire tour group stepped aside as he passed. Moreover, they returned his smile.

He reached out to shake hands. "You must be Liko?"

"Yes." Liko diffidently shook the man's hand.

"I'm your Uncle Keahi." He placed a lei of green ti leaves around Liko's neck—just like in the picture on his T-shirt— and gave Liko a hug and kissed him on both cheeks.

Liko could feel the strength in the man's handshake and hug, and even his kiss was strong. Liko felt embarrassed. His own handshake was weak. And the kiss....

"Aloha. Welcome to Hawaii."

As they waited for his luggage at carousel, Liko studied his uncle's face: a broad, flat nose, dark tanned skin, thick black eyebrows and lashes—all familiar family traits. Thick black hair, too. Yes, he had the Koholua genes of his family. However, this man carried his large-framed body with pride.

CHAPTER THREE

THE GYM WAS ON THE SECOND FLOOR of the beachside hotel, up the escalator to a reception desk where gym staff checked membership cards. The weight machines were crowded together, but a wall of windows overlooked Kuhio Beach and provided a fantastic view of the setting sun.

Carol, lying on a weight bench, raised two twenty-pound dumbbells in a wide arc until they met directly above her chest. The metal dumbbells clanged as she tapped them together. Then she lowered them below the level of the bench, slowly, working her chest.

Keahi knelt on one leg beside her and looked down, directly into her face. Carol was Chinese-European. With her shoulder-length, straight, black hair and large, almond-shaped, brown eyes, she was exotic, and very masculine. Thirty-six years old, athletic, tanned and fit, she wore tight red shorts over a black Spandex bodysuit. An emerald earring sparkled on her right ear—a gift from Keahi.

As she struggled with her seventh repetition, Keahi smiled down at her, placed his hands beneath her elbows, and prepared to help. "Looking strong!"

Carol squeezed her pectoral muscles, and again the dumbbells flew in an arc and clanged together—a little louder this time, a little less muscle control. The dumbbells wobbled above her chest.

"Two more," Keahi ordered.

Carol slowly lowered the dumbbells, and Keahi watched her chest muscles stretch underneath the tight-fitting Spandex.

Her taut stomach rose into the air as her lower back rose off the black leather bench. "Focus! Keep your back against the bench! That's good. Now hug an angel."

Keahi smiled after he said 'hug an angel' because it was their joke; Carol's girlfriend was named Angelica.

With intense focus, Carol raised the dumbbells, again in a wide arc. Keahi's large hands waited just beneath her elbows, his strength ready to help. At the top of the arc, she paused for a moment and then tapped the metal dumbbells together. They wobbled.

"One more," Keahi demanded, again encouraging her.

Determined, she lowered the dumbbells slowly.

"Keep your elbows bent. Good. That's good. Very good."

Carol groaned, and then in total concentration she arched the dumbbells upward until her strength began to fail. Keahi gave her a slight boost with the palms of his hands pushing her elbows. Her arms shook, but the dumbbells continued upward and clanged.

She sprang from the bench and returned the dumbbells to the rack next to a wall of mirrors.

Glancing at her svelte reflection—narrow waist, flat stomach, trim thighs—Carol flexed her tanned quadriceps. She shifted her weight onto her left leg and twisted her hip at an angle to the mirror. Gripping her right wrist, she worked her arms together and watched her pumped-up chest muscles ripple.

Carol smiled and her silver braces flashed back. Always improving herself, she had started bodybuilding at the age of sixteen. She had been sculpting her body for twenty years. Now she was straightening her teeth.

Normally Keahi would have commented on her most muscular pose, or he would have teased her about her braces, but today he was preoccupied and said nothing. In silence they crossed the gym to the bench press area.

He sat down on a weight bench with his back to the wall of windows, the ocean and the sunset. He appeared disoriented, as if he had forgotten where the weight plates were racked.

"You okay?"

Lost in thought, Keahi gave no answer.

"Hey, when's your nephew arriving?" she asked, raising her voice.

"He's here already."

Her brows lowered and she shot back, "Already here?"

"Yeah, his flight got in yesterday."

"What? And you didn't bring him to the gym? I expect to meet him, you know."

"Hey, I'm sorry."

"I *do* expect to meet him," the tone of her voice was emphatic.

"I had to work today," Keahi said, defending himself. "I came here straight from work." He was surprised at the whiny sound of his own voice.

Carol looked at him incredulously. "You spent the day working? It's your nephew's first day in Hawaii and you spent the day working?"

Keahi fended off her admonition. "There was an explosion. Didn't you hear about it? It's been on the radio."

"So?"

"At Kehena Kare."

"A child care center?"

"Yeah, in Kehena. I got a call this morning. At seven. They asked me to come in and cover the office while my coworker investigated the explosion."

"What happened?" Carol asked, placing a red plate on the Olympic bar Keahi was about to lift.

"A fire and an explosion—an access cover blew off an underground electrical vault in a playground." Keahi paused as if he had snapped a mental picture of the explosion and was waiting for it to digitize in his mind. "Can you imagine? A heavy metal plate flying through the air in a playground?"

"Were any children hurt?"

"Two—one burned bad, the other in shock. Fortunately, it happened late last night. The center was closed and no other kids were around."

"What were two kids doing in the playground that late at night?"

Keahi shrugged.

Carol placed another red plate on the opposite side of the Olympic bar. Keahi lay down on the bench and lifted the bar off the rack and over his chest, gracefully. Warming up, he pumped the 155 pounds up and down against the midline of his chest several times—quickly, smoothly, easily.

As he returned the bar to the rack, he let it drop. It slammed into the bar support, located above and behind his head.

Carol jumped—Keahi *never* let the weights slam.

He sprang to his feet and the sunset framed his tanned body. Behind him, the setting sun touched the ocean and the sky was awash in red and yellow and orange, all bleeding together into a rusty color.

"So where's your nephew now?"

"I don't know," he shrugged. "Hopefully at home."

Keahi looked at Carol and added, "His suitcase was stolen."

"No!"

"Right off the carousel."

"That's terrible!"

"Someone walked off with it."

"Welcome to paradise, eh?"

Keahi remembered how upset Liko had been. "Everything he had was in that suitcase."

"In one suitcase?"

"Yep, that's what he said."

"Why bring all his stuff?"

"Yeah, I had the same question. He's only supposed to be here for the summer, you know!"

Angelica entered the bench press room: 44 years old and Junoesque; blonde hair twined in a French braid; an emerald earring complementing her regal, green eyes; a sensuous mouth; and a freckled body in a black Spandex bodysuit. No gym shorts.

"Hi guys," Angelica said.

"Hello sweet," Carol replied.

Seeing them together, Keahi smiled. "Howsit, freckles?"

"Fine, big guy."

Carol grabbed another red weight plate and slid it onto the Olympic bar. Angelica followed her lead and balanced the weight on the opposite side. Now there were four large plates.

Smiling back at Keahi, Angelica said, "Let's pump some iron, you big whale!"

Keahi flinched, then gave her a coy look, with a half grin. She knew that he didn't like to be called 'big whale.' But then, he knew that she didn't like to be called 'freckles' either. He enjoyed teasing her; with her rosy brown skin tones she had always burned easily or freckled.

He lay on the bench and smoothly raised the bar across his forehead and over his chest. Then he pumped the 265 pounds up and down eight times and racked the bar.

Angelica and Carol slid on more dead weight—two yellow plates. And then Angelica ordered, "Les' go, Moby! You big hapa-whale."

"You remember what happened the last time someone teased me?"

Angelica's eyes, as green as her earring, sparkled.

Keahi had grabbed Carol by the calves, just above her ankles, and dunked her into the surf, upside down, repeatedly, until she yelled uncle. It had all been in fun, and Keahi was careful not to hurt her, and she *had* been teasing him, though now he couldn't remember about what. However, Carol's calves had been black and blue for weeks.

He had regretted that. He had a powerful grip. *It is so easy to hurt people*, he thought to himself.

Even now he twitched, recalling those bruises.

He grasped the bar, lifted the dead weight off the rack, and held it above his chest. He lowered it deliberately to an imaginary line drawn across his nipples, then he pressed it back up. He completed five more reps and racked the weights quietly.

"Look, Moby's all pumped up," Angelica said, continuing to tease him.

He frowned. "I'm *pau*," he said, jumping up. He grabbed his hand towel, keys, and water bottle off the floor.

"So what's bothering you?" Angelica asked.

He didn't answer.

"An explosion at a child care center," Carol volunteered. "And he had to work on his day off. And his nephew's luggage was stolen."

"My God." Angelica stared at him with evident concern.

"And I saved the worst for last," Carol went on. "He doesn't know what to do with his nephew—instant parent, instant crisis. And where did he go after work? Did he go straight home? No. He came here to the gym. Why?"

"Because the Big Whale's afraid of parenting?"

"Got that right," Keahi said, frowning as he walked across the room and disappeared through the door to the men's locker room.

When Keahi stepped out in front of the red Mustang convertible, he was thinking about Liko. Every year his nephew had asked permission to spend his summer vacation in Hawaii, and every year Keahi had turned him down. It had become increasingly hard to come up with a good excuse to say no, so this year Keahi had dreamed up the idea of approving the vacation, but only if his nephew became scuba certified. He never imagined that Liko would actually learn to dive. He lived in the desert for God's sake! In the desert!

And now what was he going to do with a teenage boy for a whole summer? Scuba dive? He hadn't done that in years.

The piercing blast of the horn penetrated his preoccupied mind, and he instinctively jumped back onto the sidewalk. The convertible screeched to a stop directly in front of him. An assortment of brightly colored shopping bags flew up from the backseat, landing everywhere in the car.

The driver, a middle-aged Japanese woman in silver-tinted sport sunglasses, sat rigid, gripping the steering wheel. Her reflector sunglasses hung precariously on the end of her nose, and a yellow sun visor sat cockeyed on her forehead. She frowned at Keahi, straightened her sunglasses and visor, and then drove on.

Keahi looked around. Tourists, startled by the car's horn and the screeching rubber, were staring at him. It was probably the only horn sounded in Waikiki that day.

Jolted back to the present, he walked over to the crosswalk. This time he would wait for the light to change. Tourists in cars, loud rental mopeds, and white limousines passed in front of him, bumper-to-bumper and filling all four lanes of the one-way Kalakaua Avenue.

Keahi looked across the avenue. Locals were seated at concrete game tables, playing mahjong and chess and cards under a brown, flat-roofed pavilion. A tourist leaned against a concrete column to watch. A few other tourists sat on the recycled, heavy plastic benches that had been provided recently by the City and County of Honolulu as an improvement to Waikiki.

Keahi gazed beyond the dull gray benches, out towards the ocean. He saw a few sunbathers and a handful of swimmers inside the protective reef. A lifeguard watched from a gray tower. The sun had set and most vacationers had already left Kuhio beach and had gone back to their hotels.

As he waited for the light to change, Keahi noticed a lonely palm tree growing from a small man-made hole in the wide sidewalk. He frowned at the beach improvements: man-made waterfalls, small areas of manicured grass, Caribbean tropical foliage, a wide slate rock sidewalk. The entire beach area was artificial. Even the sand had been pumped in from offshore, or trucked in by the local cement company, or from only God knew where.

The streetlight finally changed and Keahi crossed the wide avenue to the game pavilion.

Being in no hurry to go home, he stopped and watched two mahjong players—an elderly man of Chinese ancestry and an older black man. The black man sported an Atlanta Braves baseball cap, a polo shirt with small green logo on the breast pocket, tan shorts and Nike running shoes. He chain-smoked cigarettes as he played his game.

Keahi studied the black guy, who was smiling and seemed to be winning. Keahi saw few black men in Waikiki, especially black mahjong players. The man nervously tapped a mahjong tile against a small wooden box: tap-tap-tap. At the same time, his legs were pumping up and down like the pistons of an engine, keeping a sixteen-beat count. His slippers lay on the ground beside his nervous feet. He was a tightly wired little man who looked like he could explode at any moment.

At another table two guys were rapidly moving chess pieces, timing their moves with a metronome.

Keahi looked up the sidewalk. He saw tourists in designer swimsuits and local kids carrying short surfboards. He saw a group of Japanese tourists, casually dressed, walking together like a school of fish, each wearing a bright purple T-shirt.

Keahi heard a chess player push the metronome button: tap, click, click, click.

Then, a block away, Keahi saw a boy grab a purse from a middle-aged, smartly dressed Japanese tourist. Keahi watched as the local boy yanked the purse with such force that he pulled the woman to the ground. She held on to the purse and he dragged her 10 feet across rough flagstone.

When she finally let go, the purse snatcher sprinted down the sidewalk towards the game players and Keahi. Keahi heard the rhythmic click-click-click of the metronome, but everything was now happening in slow motion.

The players had heard the woman scream and they paused their games: chess pieces and mahjong tiles and playing cards were suspended above the game boards as the players turned to watch the purse snatcher sprint towards them.

The boy sprinted down the sidewalk, clutching the purse close to his chest as if it were a football. He passed within two feet of Keahi, who remained motionless. The thief then ran across the wide avenue—weaving in and out of traffic—and disappeared into the entrance of a hotel.

All eyes turned to Keahi. Why had he not stopped the purse snatcher? He was twice the size of the thief. Moreover, his muscles were still pumped and his T-shirt was still soaked with sweat and he looked stronger than a brick wall. Yet he had not stopped the thief.

Keahi read the surprise and disappointment on the old men's faces, *What is wrong with him?* Their stares stung like the tentacles of a box jellyfish.

Keahi looked back up the sidewalk to where the woman still lay with blood on the front of her stylish yellow dress. Blood was on her lower lip, and one of her cheeks was scraped. Her face had slammed into the flagstone, and Keahi wondered if her front teeth had broken.

Other Japanese tourists stood by, confused. They were not used to such violence. Moreover, the Waikiki police substation was within sight of the blood soaking into the flagstone.

Keahi heard a mahjong tile slap down onto the concrete table. He gazed at the black man's hand, too embarrassed to look into his face. Instead, he turned and began his walk home.

After about a block, his legs began to shake. For a moment he thought he'd have to sit down. Nevertheless, he continued walking, and once he reached the rainbow shower tree half a block from the Honolulu Zoo, the shaking passed. Overhead, yellow and pink pea-shaped flowers hung in masses on the sterile, hybrid tree.

Walking on, he passed homeless people on the public benches beneath the hanging branches of two large Banyan trees, or what Keahi called the *kuewan* trees. *Kuewan* was Hawaiian for homeless. The homeless were always there.

He paused in front of the bronze statue of Mahatma Gandhi, India's pacifist freedom fighter. The statue appeared so lifelike that Keahi had often imagined Gandhi stepping down off his pedestal and strolling with him on the sidewalk alongside the zoo. Now he wished that he could borrow Gandhi's bamboo staff, or lean on his bony shoulder.

He asked himself, *Should I have stopped the thief? I could have clotheslined him. But what if I had broken his neck?*

At 7:30pm, Keahi peered through the glass louvers and screen of his front door into his studio apartment on Pualai Circle and saw Liko sitting on the green sofa behind the coffee table. The bluish light from the television reflected off Liko's white T-shirt and softly illuminated his face.

Keahi opened the door and stepped into the hallway that separated the U-shaped kitchen on his left from the small bathroom on his right. He took three steps straight ahead to the end of the short hallway and stopped at the entrance to the studio, a cramped room that was both a television area and a bedroom space. On his left were the small flat-screened television, a coffee table, and Liko, sitting on a large green sofa. On his right was a queen size bed. A golden-yellow Japanese folding screen divided the television area from the Koa wood bed.

"Hello, Liko."

Keahi tossed his gym bag onto the bed behind the screen. He opened a sliding screen door and stepped out onto the lanai that ran the length of the studio. He grabbed a blue and white striped lounge chair off the lanai and returned. Keahi placed the lounge chair across from the television, settled in, and asked, "How was your first day in Hawaii?"

"Okay, I guess," Liko replied. "I'm hungry."

"How does *brok da mouf* stew sound?"

"Interesting." Liko made the mistake of raising his voice, which boomed off the bare-finished, concrete walls and concrete ceiling. "It sounds interesting."

Keahi got up from the lounge chair and walked into the narrow U-shaped kitchen. In seven steps he could be anyplace in his studio.

He opened the small white refrigerator door and found a beige bowl sitting by itself on the top wire shelf. After removing the Tupperware and popping the airtight lid, he spooned the thick beef stew into a sauce pan on the electric stove. He wiped stew drippings off the stovetop and, as he threw the soiled paper towel away, he noticed in the trash can an empty bottle of wine. He paused and turned his head in the direction of Liko in the other room. The large bottle had been unopened when he left for work. It wasn't expensive, but it wasn't cheap, either.

He walked back into the television area holding the empty bottle. "Your dad liked the wine too," he said, giving Liko the stink eye.

The effect was immediate, as if Liko had been slapped.

"I'm not my dad," he objected. "We have nothing in common."

Keahi took a half step back. "You can drink, but only inside this studio," he warned. "Understand?"

Liko nodded.

"And you are not allowed to get drunk—period. When you drink, drink moderately, a couple or three beers, a couple glasses of wine. Understand?"

"Yes," Liko said, his voice low.

"Okay then," Keahi said firmly.

After a pause he added, "The stew will be ready in a few minutes."

He stepped over to his bed and ruffled through his gym bag. He pulled out a plastic grocery bag containing his wet swimsuit and a damp towel. "I'm taking a quick shower."

In the bathroom, he dropped the wine bottle into the waste basket between the sink and the toilet.

He hung the damp towel on a hook on the back of the bathroom door, which he then closed. Next, he rinsed the salt water out of the swimsuit into the hand sink, and then hung the suit over the neck of the showerhead. Finally he took off his gym clothes and stepped into the light brown tiled shower and turned on the cold water. He enjoyed shivering in a cold shower. As he worked shampoo into his thick black hair, he thought, *I hope Liko doesn't have a drinking problem.*

After Liko had watched half an episode of a reality

show, Keahi reappeared, wearing dark blue shorts and an old, longboards T-shirt. His thick, black hair was wet and combed straight back over his head. He was barefoot.

He handed Liko a red bowl of hot stew and some soda crackers. He reached behind Liko and turned on the standing brass lamp.

Liko flinched under the incandescent bulb, his eyes bloodshot, his face puffy.

He has my sister's fiery eyes, Keahi thought as he sat down in the lounge chair and set his dinner on his lap. The bowl of stew was steaming hot, so Keahi got up and turned up the Casablanca ceiling fan directly overhead. He also picked up the Honolulu Star Bulletin from the coffee table, folded it, and set it between the hot dish and his lap.

Keahi wondered if Liko had read the paper. It contained an article about the explosion at the child care center, including a photograph of the playground—but Keahi didn't mention it. He didn't want to talk about work. Instead, he wanted to learn something about this sixteen-year-old kid sitting on his sofa. Or was he seventeen now?

He took a long look at Liko. He was wearing baggy shorts, a white T-shirt, and white socks with leather slippers. *He needs to lose the socks*, Keahi thought. *And he needs to work on his tan. He's so pale he's haole white!*

Looking around the apartment, Keahi wondered what Liko thought of his few belongings. The brass lamp was from Korea, made from brass shell casings left behind by Americans after the Korean War. The solid Koa bed and solid Koa mirror behind the Japanese screen were a gift from his aunt. She had purchased them from a local craftsman.

When Keahi moved out of her home she had bought him a bedroom set. The set had included a Koa wood dresser too, but that was now stored at his aunt's because it was too large for the studio.

The studio satisfied all his basic needs: a place to sleep, eat, and rest. And he could watch the sunset from the lanai, and then the moon and stars as he drank.

He had little desire for material goods, although the few pieces he owned were very nice. The large coffee table was Birdseye maple with a brass edging. Keahi had found it at a garage sale. A *haole*, returning to the mainland, had parted with it for a fraction of its value. Keahi wondered if Liko would appreciate the quality of the wood and the unusual, large swirling eyes peering from the smooth grain.

The four-panel Japanese screen was a gift from his late boyfriend, Daniel. A black wooden edging framed a hand-painted mountain scene set against a golden background. Keahi read the scene from right to left: the first panel showed an old fisherman, followed closely by a small boy, hiking along a coastal trail, carrying cane fishing poles; the second panel showed a frothing stream entering the ocean; the third panel showed paths along the coast and a path entering the mountains; and the final panel showed cascading waterfalls. The golden background reflected the light from the standing brass lamp that was behind Liko.

The green sleeper sofa that Liko was sitting on had an interior metal frame and was so heavy that the original owner had paid Keahi to haul it away. In fact, Keahi had trouble moving it. It had a gold brocade pattern of leaves. No one made furniture like that any more.

All in all, I'm well-off, Keahi thought to himself. *I have enough stuff.* He wondered what Liko thought, though.

During a commercial, he picked up his bamboo nose flute, his *'ohe hano ihu.*

"I tried to play it," Liko commented, "but I had no luck."

"Did you play it with your nose?" Keahi closed one nostril with his thumb and blew into the hole at the node-end of the flute. A note bounced around in the concrete confines of the studio.

"That's disgusting."

Keahi ignored the remark and played a short Hawaiian tune from a traditional song. He used to sing the song for tourists when he was a teenager, Liko's age, when he still believed in the power of music and dance. When he finished, he set the nose flute back on the bookshelf. He then carried the dirty dishes to the kitchen, and washed and set them on the dish rack to air dry. When he returned, they moved to the lanai and sat in the blue and white striped outdoor lounge chairs.

Liko wondered: *How can such a big guy live in such a small place? This place is smaller than Mom's trailer.*

He asked, "Why aren't there more coconuts?"

"Coconut trees?"

"Yeah, I thought Hawaii had lots of coconuts."

"No. We are too far north. Coconut trees grow better near the equator."

Keahi studied Liko. Could this young man really be his sister's son, and a full-blooded native Hawaiian?

"Do you like *poi*?" Keahi asked.

"I dunno." From the tone of Liko's voice, Keahi guessed that Liko had never tried it.

"Really? Your dad loved *poi*. When he lived Hawaii, he ate it plenty."

Keahi noted that Liko's face went blank.

"*Poi* is pounded taro root," Keahi explained. "It's sticky and purple and tastes bland. In the past, our ancestors ate lots of it."

"I know what it is," Liko said.

Keahi got up and went inside to get a wooden board and pestle off the top shelf. He returned and sat down. "This is a *poi* board and a *poi* pounder. A *pohaku ku'i*." Keahi held up the large pestle. As he spoke the Hawaiian words, he noticed that Liko's eyes glazed over. He also noticed that Liko had trouble focusing on the *poi* pounder.

"Do you surf?"

"I've never tried."

"Do you fish?"

"No," Liko said, growing irritated. "Look, I live in the desert. There's no ocean, no lakes."

"Well, at least you can scuba."

"Yeah, I learned in an abandoned quarry."

Keahi watched a troubled expression cross Liko's face.

"Yes, I got my certification."

"Good. Very good, because this weekend we're going to Hanauma Bay with some friends. You'll like it. Hanauma Bay is a nature reserve. The fish swim right up to you."

"Diving?"

"No, snorkeling. There's a lot to see snorkeling. We can dive another weekend."

"I'd much rather dive," Liko said, knowing that he needed the floatation of his dive jacket to stay afloat.

"We will, soon enough. I've enrolled us in an advanced scuba class." Keahi had decided to enroll them both because it was a way for him to brush up on his own scuba skills and hopefully Liko would find it fun. "It starts in three weeks. In the meantime, we'll snorkel at Hanauma Bay and you can get acquainted with the local marine life. You'll like it."

When Keahi had said 'advanced,' Liko's palms had begun to sweat. He now wiped them on his shorts.

They were silent for a while. Then Keahi said, "Remind me to tell you the story about the time your dad and I went diving off Lahaina, looking for the U.S.S. Bluegill, a World War II sub. She was scuttled years ago a couple hundred yards off shore."

Liko didn't say anything.

"In the old days, when your dad and I dived together, divers got hurt looking for that sub. Some died."

Liko was silent.

"Did you buy a new toothbrush?" Keahi asked, suddenly remembering that all of Liko's stuff had been stolen.

"No."

Keahi recalled how upset Liko had been at the airport when he discovered that his suitcase had been stolen.

"Well, tomorrow we can stop by Longs Drug and pick up whatever you need."

Liko remained silent.

"I know it's tough losing all your stuff," Keahi said. "I'll buy you whatever you need for the summer." *And you'll return home with a better wardrobe*, he thought.

Keahi suddenly felt irritated at Liko's silence.

"Tomorrow we've got a busy day," he said. "We'll see the Arizona Memorial and the Bowfin submarine and Punchbowl Crater. And then we will do the shopping."

Silence.

"Well, I guess its time to turn in," he said. "We need to get up early, start our day at five."

Later, as he lay in bed watching the whirling teak blades on the Casablanca ceiling fan, Keahi wondered what was wrong with Liko. He hoped Liko's quiet mood was not his usual personality but just a reaction to the wine. He didn't like trying to carry on a conversation by himself. He expected conversation, or at least an attempt at conversation.

Drinking that whole bottle of wine was stupid, Keahi thought. *Does he lack self control or does he have a drinking problem – or both!*

And Liko, on the other side of the folding screen, lying quietly on the hide-a-way bed, was also watching the ceiling fan. But he was dejected. *How can I snorkel when I can barely swim? At least when I dive, the jacket keeps me afloat.*

The ceiling fan was making an annoying noise.

And all my money was in that suitcase! Liko moaned to himself. *No money, no apartment. No money, no senior year in Hawaii.*

But that's not what had embarrassed him. Earlier in the day, when he had strolled down to the beach by himself to check out the territory, the waves and the babes, fate had taken him to the aptly named Queens Beach, the beach where men sunbathed for the enjoyment of other men. But it was not their sunbathing that had embarrassed him.

What embarrassed him was the fact that he was the most overweight body on the beach.

That's why, later, when he returned to the studio, he had drunk the whole bottle of Malbec. The first sip reasserted himself and his pride. He had been so embarrassed at the beach that he had not even taken off his T-shirt. Each subsequent sip made him feel better and better, until he quickly finished the whole bottle and collapsed onto the carpet, just short of passing out.

All afternoon he had lain there, on his back, watching the fan blades turn and turn and turn. With each revolution he fought himself not to throw up. It was one of the most miserable afternoons of his life.

Now as he lay on the sleeper sofa he was again watching the blades, but this time he was feeling miserable because Keahi had compared him to his dad. *I'm nothing like my dad,* he thought, angrily.

CHAPTER FOUR

KEAHI STOOD IN THE CENTRAL OBSERVATION area of the Arizona Memorial Monument and looked overhead at the American flag hanging limply against the blue Hawaiian sky. It was early morning. The temperature had already risen into the high seventies, and the trade winds had failed; Keahi knew it was going to be a hot, still, uncomfortable day. Standing in the bright sunlight, he already felt sticky. He plucked at the center of his T-shirt, repeatedly lifting it off his chest, fanning himself. Sweat trickled down his lower back.

He wasn't thinking about the dead sailors aboard the sunken battleship, which rested peacefully in the ocean below him. Instead, he was thinking about the two boys who had been hurt Sunday night in the fire and explosion. One boy was badly burned and was in critical condition at Kaiser Hospital. He would probably die. The other boy was catatonic and had been moved to Saint Francis. The newspapers said he was expected to make a full recovery. *The boy's parents must be going through hell*, Keahi thought.

How does a playground catch fire and explode? The chief fire inspector, quoted in the Honolulu Advertiser, had said the fire was "not deliberately set," yet he did not identify its cause. And a police officer, also quoted in the same article, had agreed. "Just a freak accident," he had said. But neither had explained the origin of the fire.

Keahi thought, *I should be at work helping Picric Pete, not sightseeing.* Feeling guilty, he turned to Liko and snapped, "Did you lock your car door?"

Liko looked at him as if he had lost his mind. They were standing on the Arizona Memorial and the car was a long way away—a shuttle boat ride to the museum and then a five-minute walk to the parking lot. Liko thought, *He's still pissed about the wine.*

Together they walked across the breadth of the Memorial, working their way through a large group of Japanese tourists. When they reached the railing they looked over the side and saw the sunken U.S.S. Arizona directly below them, lying perpendicular to the memorial.

Droplets of oil rose from the battleship and formed an iridescent sheen, like a metallic rainbow floating on the water: rusty brown and yellow and lavender.

Liko closed his eyes. He imagined smoke billowing skyward, the smell of diesel burning, the surprise that the sailors had felt, the fear and the horror as their ship exploded and sank.

Keahi stared at Liko. He was gripping the railing so tightly, his knuckles had turned white. Beads of perspiration covered his forehead and his eyes were closed.

"Are you okay?"

Liko opened his eyes. "Yes," he answered, but his voice sounded weak. "I'm fine."

"I just heard a tour guide say that sailors are entombed below," he added, "inside the battleship. I didn't realize this is a tomb."

"It was a surprise attack. Half the men who died, died aboard this battleship."

"Were any trapped alive?"

"I don't know," Keahi said. "Sailors aboard the U.S.S. Virginia were trapped alive. Some lived for days."

They walked to the far end of the monument and entered a room where the names of the men who died were inscribed in black letters on a white marble wall. The names filled the entire wall from the floor to the ceiling.

Liko read an inscription: "To the memory of the gallant men here entombed and their shipmates who gave their lives in action on December 7, 1941 on the U.S.S. Arizona."

The shrine room was shady and cool and quiet.

To the right of Keahi, Liko saw an old Japanese man bow deeply in the direction of a wreath of flowers hung on a white tripod in front of the marble wall. His bow was slow and conveyed deep respect.

Behind them, Liko heard laughing and loud talking. He turned around and faced a gaggle of young tourists, both Japanese and American, who were pushing their way inside. The venerable old man also turned. He stretched out his hand towards the Japanese tourists and made cutting motions in the air. "Shitsurei shimasu." They stepped aside like the Red Sea parting. The old man passed through and exited the room. Liko and Keahi followed.

Once outside, the old Japanese man walked across the deck to the distant railing, stopping where the deck overlooked the sunken battleship. They watched as he removed the plumeria lei from around his neck. He broke the lei and slid his finger slowly down the string, stripping white flowers off one at a time. The yellow-throated blossoms fell onto the surface of the ocean and floated away on the iridescent sheen.

After that, Keahi and Liko wandered around the observation area, Keahi thinking about the child care explosion, Liko thinking about the girl who drowned in the quarry.

Eventually they made their way back to the shady room where they had entered the memorial. Before he got in line to reboard the shuttle boat, however, Liko touched the warm metal of a large brass bell, which hung from a wooden beam. The bell was engraved 'U.S.S. Arizona 1916.'

A few minutes later, everyone stepped into the bright sunlight, boarded the shuttle boat, and returned to the museum.

It was two hours before lunch when Keahi and Liko stopped at the hot dog vendor's cart outside the privately operated U.S.S. Bowfin Submarine Museum. After finishing large Cokes and a plumper with the works, Keahi purchased tickets.

As they walked across the boarding bridge to the deck of the gray submarine, Keahi read her hull number out loud: "Ol' Two Eighty Seven. She's as long as a football field."

And as wide as a double-wide trailer, Liko thought.

Once aboard, they descended the rungs of a metal ladder into the belly of the Bowfin, passing from bright sunlight into the dim incandescent light of sparsely spaced overhead bulbs. Surface sounds disappeared. Stagnant air filled their lungs.

When they reached the forward torpedo room, Keahi turned to Liko and noticed that he had again turned pale and perspiration had again broken out on his forehead.

"Everything okay?"

Liko swept the beads of sweat off his forehead with the fingers of his right hand. "I'm fine." He wiped his hand across the front of his shorts, leaving a dark mark of perspiration. Descending the steps had reminded him of his descent into the flooded quarry, and that had reminded him of the drowned girl.

"Don't bump your head on the low hatchways," someone said. Glancing behind him, Keahi saw an enlisted sailor dressed in uniform, wearing a badge on his left breast pocket. The badge was a silver eagle surrounded by three inverted silver stars, above several inverted V-shaped stripes. Keahi had no idea what his rank was.

"Thanks," Keahi offered.

The sailor was in his forties, muscular, with a high and tight military haircut, and a well-groomed black moustache. Keahi liked the moustache.

"This was the place to be," the sailor offered. "The crew watched movies in this room."

Keahi stretched out his arms from one side of the Bowfin to the other, touching the cold bodies of two black torpedoes. The torpedoes had shiny brass noses. He counted six torpedo chambers—two stacks of three. One torpedo was loaded.

"How large was her crew?" he asked.

"During war patrols? Ten officers. Seventy men."

Keahi tried to imagine 80 men living aboard this small vessel. What he imagined wasn't a comfortable picture.

He ran his beefy hand down a smooth black torpedo and caressed its shiny brass nose. Then he squatted and peered into a shiny brass chamber where a red light glowed deep within. He stood up and looked over at the sailor, as if he expected him to provide an explanation for an unasked question.

"She officially sank sixteen ships. That includes six men-of-war and a Vichy French pilot ship."

"A Vichy ship?" a tourist standing next to Liko asked. "What's that?"

"A French ship. The crew of the Bowfin sank her off the coast of Vietnam, near Saigon. The Vichy French ship was escorting a Japanese convoy into port."

"The Japanese fought in the Vietnam War?" Liko asked.

"No, no," the sailor said, correcting Liko. "The Vichy Ship was sunk during World War II."

"That was before he was born," Keahi said to the sailor with a smile. "Wasn't it, Liko?"

"Yeah, my father fought in Vietnam. I was born after that."

And I was a conscientious objector, Keahi thought to

himself. He had avoided the draft by attending the University of Hawaii. Liko's father, on the other hand, had never been good with the books; consequently, he had done a tour of Vietnam. And he had returned with a serious alcohol problem.

"How long could she stay submerged?" Liko asked.

"Not long by today's standards. Technically, she's not even a submarine. She has no climate control, no nuclear propulsion. She could stay submerged only a short time. Today's nuclear-powered submarines, like the U.S.S. Abraham Lincoln, they can stay submerged for two months."

A tourist asked, "Are those the subs with the Trident missiles?"

"Yes, nuclear missiles. The Bowfin is World War II vintage. She carried these Mark IV torpedoes. They occasionally turned and sank the submarine that fired them."

Keahi and Liko looked at each other; Keahi raised an eyebrow.

The next compartment was the wardroom, which the officer said was located over the forward battery compartment. Keahi become interested, because he knew that working with batteries could be extremely hazardous. He asked a lot of questions and learned that there were more than a hundred batteries. When recharged—usually on the surface and at night—they gave off deadly hydrogen gas, which was extremely explosive; indeed, the tiniest spark could ignite the gas and cripple the submarine, or rip her apart.

"Were there any accidents?" Keahi asked.

"No," the sailor answered. "Not aboard this ship. There was an accident with batteries aboard the U.S.S. F-4, a submarine that operated out of Honolulu Harbor a long time ago—around the time of World War I, 1915 or so."

"What happened?"

"Sea water entered her battery compartment. Most of her crew fled to the engine room to get away from the fire and the chlorine gas. She drifted downward until she imploded. All aboard died."

"How deep could the Bowfin dive before *she* imploded?" Liko asked.

"She couldn't dive much deeper than her length, which is about 300 feet."

When they came to the officers' dining room, the sailor stopped. Everyone gathered around him and looked at the dining table, which was covered with a green tablecloth embossed in gold with a picture of the bow of a submarine grasped between two fish. "This was a dining table *and* an operating table."

Liko tried to visualize a wounded sailor lying on the table, bleeding, dying. To his surprise, he recalled the image of the drowned girl, lying dead on red sandstone after she was pulled from the flooded quarry. He shook his head regretfully.

Keahi, meanwhile, was studying the yeoman's quarters. A small, black L.C. Smith typewriter sat on a three-foot wide desk. The gray metal desk had four small drawers on each side. He said, "Now this is cramped! Next time I'm feeling cramped in my cubicle at work, I'll remember how bad this sailor had it."

A while later they regrouped in front of the main gyroscope in the control room, where Liko asked the sailor, "How did she maintain buoyancy control?"

"There were forward and aft ballast tanks to maintain neutral buoyancy. The diving officer could keep the submarine suspended at a given depth, without sinking or rising. The ballast tanks were used to dive or surface. If the captain wanted to dive, the ballast tanks were filled with water. If he wanted to surface, seawater was expelled with compressed air. Expelling the sea water was known as 'blowing the ballast.'"

Keahi said to Liko, "It's the same kind of thing you do when you scuba dive, except you add air to your jacket instead of water."

"The Bowfin could add or expel tons of water," the sailor said. "Scuba divers just add or expel air."

"Buoyancy control, especially neutral buoyancy control, is critical for deep diving." Keahi looked directly at Liko to see how he reacted to this statement.

He appeared irritated, a shade paler.

"You know how to control your buoyancy?"

Liko thought about doing pushups on the wooden platform in the quarry instead of the fin pivots that had been required. He drew in a breath and hoped his voice wouldn't betray his concern as he replied, "Of course I do."

After they completed the below-deck tour, they ascended and stepped out of the Bowfin, out of the belly of the bottom feeder, and into the bright light of the afternoon sun. They thanked the officer and, after shaking hands, parted company and left the submarine.

They returned to the car. The doors were locked and neither of them said anything about that.

Keahi was enjoying himself and he was pleased with Liko's behavior, so he decided that their next stop would be Punchbowl.

Standing in an extinct volcano at the entrance to the ten Courts of the Missing, Keahi and Liko silently read the altar-like plaque:

IN THESE GARDENS ARE RECORDED
THE NAMES OF AMERICANS
WHO GAVE THEIR LIVES
IN THE SERVICE OF THEIR COUNTRY
AND WHOSE EARTHLY RESTING PLACE
IS KNOWN ONLY TO GOD

Liko saw more text inscribed on the face of a tall and wide monolith. He looked closely and discovered the names of men. His fingertips touched a name. The white marble was warm, warmed by the bright Hawaiian sun. He silently read the stranger's name.

Observing the puzzled expression on his face, Keahi said, "They're the names of soldiers who died in World War II, the Korean War, and Vietnam." After a long pause, he added, "Their bodies were never found."

"Really? None of these guys are buried here?" Liko slowly walked around the massive rectangular memorial, dragging the palm of his hand across the warm surface, feeling the edges of names. The names covered the entire surface of the monolith, and the walls were taller than he could reach, wider than he could stretch. And this massive, rectangular memorial that he had just walked around was just one of ten that flanked both sides of a stairway that climbed skyward like a Mayan temple.

The memorial is so heavy, he thought, *yet the engraved names have no weight. Without earthly remains, it all ascends to lightness!* But he said, "It would take a week to read all these names."

The faintest scent of sweet plumeria wafted in the air. Keahi inhaled it deeply as they climbed seven sets of steps from the crater floor to the Court of Honor. When they reached the top step, they turned around.

The sky had changed from clear, sunny, and hot, to trade winds and cumulus clouds. The day had grown darker and their moods doleful.

Beneath them lay a cemetery in the caldera of an extinct volcano. They saw row after row of marble grave markers, flush with the surface of the earth in a sea of green grass. Cut flowers flagged on many of the graves. The cemetery looked full.

Keahi imagined all the buried bodies and thought it ugly. *What if they all suddenly rose from the dead?* Liko, on the other hand, thought it peaceful and beautiful.

"I wonder what they believed in?" Keahi said. He thought of his unused talents: singing, dancing, and chanting. *I've devoted my life to bureaucracy. I've cultivated complacency, not interest. Not joy, not passion!*

He looked at Liko. "Is there anything that you would devote your life to? Sacrifice your life for?"

Liko didn't reply. He was out of shape, and he was still catching his breath after climbing the seven sets of steps.

The humid trade winds carried the smell of freshly cut grass. At the far side of the crater, across the green lawn and beyond the monkeypod trees, a groundskeeper was riding a lawnmower, which was humming along.

No, Liko couldn't think of anything he believed in strongly enough to die for—if that was what Keahi was asking. Yes, he wanted adventure, he wanted girls, and most especially he wanted to discover his purpose in life. But today he had no faith, no girlfriends, and no purpose other than to begin his adventure. Besides, he didn't want that kind of ambition, anyway.

They heard a jet overhead and spotted an F-22 Raptor as it slipped into a white cloud. Close behind was another Raptor, and then yet another.

"Liko, when I die, I want to be cremated and I want my ashes buried under a banyan tree, or a hau tree."

"You can put my ashes in a pepper shaker," Liko responded, flippantly.

Keahi grimaced but then laughed, relieved to have the tension broken, finally.

"Ho," Liko said, pleased that Keahi had laughed. "Not da small manini kine like picnic or home li'dat, but da kine beeg kine."

"So you speak pidgin?"

"Eh, muddah talk pidgin wen . . . when she gets drunk."

"I see."

Liko watched the lawnmower circle around a monkey pod tree. "She gets drunk a lot."

Keahi was saddened to hear that, nevertheless he took the opportunity to make a joke. "So you're fluent in pidgin, then?"

Liko smiled. "Uncle, you're all right."

"Well, Liko, I'm glad you think so. But I have to tell you—if you drink wine again like you did last night, I'm going to put you on a plane straight back to Las Vegas. You understand?"

Fair enough, Liko thought. And in rebellion against his mom and dad, both of whom were alcoholics, he nodded, yes.

"Okay, then. Let's take a look at the city."

They followed the memorial walk to an overlook at the far rim of the crater. Before them sprawled Honolulu: unplanned, hot concrete and iron and glass, in front of the blue ocean. In the distance was Waikiki, a tourist city in the Pacific. And then Diamond Head. Diamond Head was almost hidden behind the tall buildings that flanked both sides of the Ala Wai Canal. And the canal was barely visible, too. It lay dead and decaying like the body of an anaconda, decapitated and stretched-out along the full length of Waikiki. Most of the buildings were high-rise condominiums with attached lanais, old and boxy. The buildings looked like gnawed corncobs.

Keahi said, "Waikiki is an overdeveloped resort, created by engineers who drained the wetlands. It's really just an over-hyped resort where elderly tourists spend a lot of money."

Liko thought, *Whoever built Honolulu must have hated the ocean, the mountains, and the local trade winds.*

"It's hard to believe now, but Hawaiians used to live in Waikiki. They grew taro and raised mullet in fish ponds. Kaahumanu, one of the early Hawaiian chiefs, had his royal home on Waikiki Beach. Last night you were asking about coconuts? Well, Kaahumanu planted the first coconut trees. It's said they grew into a grove of tens of thousands of trees."

"When was that?"

"Oh, probably about the time that Columbus was discovering the Bahamas." Keahi smiled.

Liko gazed out from the lookout. There were no coconut trees in sight, just concrete, glass and asphalt.

"Waikiki used to be a wetland, a place for ducks and fish and taro and rice. Then the Culex mosquito was introduced, sometime in the early 1800's. After that Waikiki became a miserable place to visit. It was certainly not a place you wanted to live. You could lose more blood living in Waikiki than—"

"Where did the mosquitoes come from?" Liko interrupted.

"The merchant ships. About a hundred years before that, Kamehameha had invaded. He was a chief from the island of Hawaii. He was power-hungry and blood-thirsty and ruthless.

"His army landed at Kuhio Beach and killed the chief of Oahu, Kalanikupule, a descendant of the chief who planted all the coconuts.

"A fierce battle started on Kuhio Beach, near where I go to the gym. Kalanikupule's army retreated here to Punchbowl. In fact, some warriors died here. Right where we are standing, probably. Some retreated farther into Nuuanu Valley." Keahi pointed up the valley into the mountains.

"Some were driven to the Pali and forced off the cliffs. They fell to their deaths, you know."

"I'd like to see it," Liko said.

Why? Keahi wondered. *It's a memorial to human savagery.* He gazed towards Waikiki and the ocean.

"Shortly after he conquered this island, Kamehameha gathered his army on the beach at Waikiki. He planned to conquer Kauai, too, but before he set sail, a plague, possibly cholera, killed many of his warriors. So you know what he did?"

Liko shook his head.

"He offered a sacrifice to his gods."

"A human sacrifice?"

"Two men."

"Where?"

"On the beach at Waikiki."

Keahi was silent for a moment while he recalled the details that his teachers had taught him. "Their arms and legs were broken. Their eyes were scooped out. And they were thrown into a hut, overnight. With multiple broken bones and no eyes, they were unable to escape."

Liko was listening intently.

"The next day they were placed on an altar in a *heiau* near the beach and beaten to death with clubs."

Keahi studied Liko for a moment and then continued. "Many years ago there was a *heiau*, a temple, here too."

"Here?" Liko asked.

"Yes, right here—our ancestors offered human sacrifices to their god, *Ku,* here on the rim of this volcano."

"You mean they would bring people up here and club them to death?"

"No, no." Keahi was amused at Liko's interest. "They didn't always club 'em to death. Sometimes they burned 'em."

Liko's jaw dropped. "Alive? They burned them alive?"

"Not always. Sometimes they drowned 'em first."

Liko shook his head, astounded.

"This is *Pu'owaina*, Hill of Sacrifice. The priests drowned their victims and then carried them up here to an *imu ahi*, a fire oven, on the rim of this volcano. The draught of air from below helped the fire burn hot."

Now, standing on the edge of the Hill of Sacrifice, Keahi closed his eyes and inhaled deeply to regain his composure. He reminded himself that it was just history—just a recurring nightmare that had troubled him through his teenage years.

Liko, however, was enthralled. He was especially interested in the warriors and wanted to know more. But Keahi became silent.

Afterwards they drove to Ala Moana Shopping Center and Keahi bought Liko a toothbrush, hairbrush and other toiletries at Longs Drug Store. In a surf shop, Keahi helped him pick out a pair of royal blue board shorts with bold gold piping to replace the baggy blue swim trunks that were lost with the stolen luggage. Liko was deeply embarrassed when he tried on the skin-tight rash guard, but Keahi insisted that he needed it to protect against the sun. The beach flip-flops were so comfortable that he wore them out of the surf shop. No more socks and sandals. At the Old Navy store he scored two pairs of light brown cargo shorts. But what impressed Liko the most was the top-of-the-line sunglasses. "They will block glare and UV," the salesman guaranteed. The brand-name was Warrior Gyms.

CHAPTER FIVE

THE NEXT MORNING AT 7:00AM, Keahi was at work in his cubicle at the Department of Energy, which had recently been renamed the Department of Water, Wind and Sun, after the three natural resources that Hawaii had in abundance. Keahi actually worked in the Hazardous Substance Cleanup Section.

Santos, his supervisor, came out of his spacious office—Santos had the only real office with a door that could be closed—and lumbered down the aisle between cubicles, passing Keahi's small work area. His untucked aloha shirt covered an enormous stomach. Santos had the girth of a short sumo wrestler but none of the muscle or coordination. His arms and legs were short and fat. He reminded Keahi of a dwarf hippo, out of water, walking upright. He stopped in front of Pete's cubicle. Pete was an emergency responder.

"Are you quitting?" he asked Pete in a heavy voice, upset.

"I found your resignation on my desk." He waved a letter in the air.

"Yes."

"Come into my office," Santos ordered.

"No." Pete's voice was calm. "Whatever you have to say, you can tell me out here."

"I want you in my office."

"No."

"Don't you think this is short notice?" Santos asked, sarcastically, his voice rising. "You just walk into work, leave a note on my desk, and quit?"

"Check the union contract. I don't have to give notice."

"That's not the point. I expected more from you."

Pete shrugged his broad shoulders.

"This is aimed at me, isn't it?" Santos made little puffing sounds. He often made little puffing sounds when he got excited. There was a pause as he caught his breath. "You're not giving me the respect I deserve."

The office was deathly still. Everyone was listening.

"I give respect to those who deserve it."

Santos waved a finger in Pete's face and said loudly, "I thought you were more professional." He turned and walked back down the row of cubicles to his office, his breathing labored. He slammed the door.

Keahi waited a moment, then ventured to Pete's cubicle and dropped into his guest chair. "What was that all about?"

"I quit."

"Are you okay?" Keahi had almost said "Are you crazy?"

"Haven't you heard? Little Bill and I walked into a meth lab." Pete cleared his throat, his blue eyes growing moist.

"And it exploded."

"It was an odor complaint," he added. "Can you believe that? Someone called in a meth lab as an odor complaint?"

Not waiting for an answer, he continued, "The arson investigator thinks there were acetone vapors. He thinks a spark from the light switch caused the explosion."

Keahi shook his head in amazement.

Pete managed a thin smile. "When I came to, I heard someone running down the stairs yelling 'earthquake!'"

Keahi shook his head again.

"The apartment must have been totally destroyed."

Pete looked around his cubicle with a vague expression, took a battered reference book off his bookcase, and dropped it absentmindedly into an empty Gordon Biersch box. He gathered up papers lying on his desk into a neat pile. Then he leaned back against the hardwood slats of his mission-style, swivel office chair and sighed.

He's exhausted, Keahi thought.

"I was standing in front of the resident manager when the place exploded. She'd unlocked the apartment door and stepped back. Little Bill stepped around us and went into the apartment first. I started to follow him and then I smelled something sweet—it must have been the acetone—and then Little Bill flicked on the lights. The door blew off its hinges and knocked me to the ground. I never heard the explosion, can you believe that? It knocked me out. I found myself lying on my back with the door on top of me. I was still holding the doorknob! Can you believe that? The door knocked the wind out of me. I couldn't catch my breath. I was lucky it was a solid door. If it had been a louvered door, the louvers would have sliced right through me like a loaf of bread. I saw the resident manager slumped against the wall behind me, across the hallway, still clutching the master keys in her hand. The explosion knocked her out, cold. They took *her* away in an ambulance."

"Little Bill . . . well, Little Bill was standing just inside the apartment when it exploded." Pete took a deep breath and sighed again. "The force of the blast knocked him against the inside of the door. I was on one side of the door, he was on the other. The blast jellied his organs. It shook and rearranged his organs. Can you believe that?"

Keahi imagined Little Bill's internal organs turned to jelly, sloughing off inside his thoracic cavity.

"He died shortly after the ambulance arrived. I was told that he never regained consciousness."

There would have been no way to save him, Keahi thought.

"I should have gone in first."

Keahi gently rested his hand on Pete's shoulder.

Pete grimaced and Keahi quickly removed his hand. "Sorry."

"That's all right. I'm just bruised all over."

After a pause he continued. "I can't think straight. Every once in a while my body starts shaking—my *whole* body." He added, "It's a strange feeling to lose control of your body."

Keahi noticed the bruises on Pete's arm.

"Yeah, my left side is one big bruise from my shoulder to my calf."

"You should be in the hospital!"

Pete smiled, half-heartedly. "The doctor wanted to give me

a tranquilizer, which I refused, of course. I just got up and walked out. Probably a stupid thing to do, right? But, here I am."

Keahi noticed Pete's hands plucking at the knees of his jeans.

"Use your sick leave and stay home a few days. Pound down a few beers. Do some sake bombs." Keahi forced a smile. "But don't quit."

"No," Pete shook his head. His disheveled, wavy-brown hair just covered his ears. "I need a different job, not time off."

Pete's hands were working again, this time smoothing the cotton cloth of his faded jeans over both knees.

"I could talk to Santos for you." Keahi stood up and looked over the top of the cubicle partition. He saw Santos standing in his office, behind his full-size picture window, talking on the phone. Santos saw him and glared at him. The hair on the back of Keahi's neck stood up.

What's the matter with him? Keahi wondered. *He's not the one who got hurt.* "I can't believe that he just marched into your cubicle and argued with you like that, especially after everything that's happened."

"He's an asshole," Pete said.

Pete's blue eyes started to fill with tears.

"Take some time off. Let things settle. Hang out at the beach. Relax. In a couple of weeks, if you still want to leave, no one will stop you."

Pete rubbed the tips of his fingers across his eyes, then he placed his hand on top of Keahi's hand, gently. He smiled. "Thanks, Keahi, but no. The time to leave is now. Help me pack a few things, will you?" His eyes surveyed his small cubicle. "I need to get out of here."

He removed a small, framed photograph from the wall above his desk. "Do you remember this?" He handed it to Keahi.

Keahi recognized it immediately. It was a picture of Pete and two Coast Guard workers seated in a yellow Zodiac boat surrounded by black oil. The oil had smeared halfway up the side of the Zodiac. Pete had black oil stains on his green coveralls, whereas the Coasties' blue coveralls were spotless, untouched by the thick oil that floated all around them in the Pearl Harbor estuary.

"I took this picture, didn't I?" Keahi asked, handing the framed picture back to Pete, who dropped it into a Dos Equis box.

"Yeah, a long time ago."

Keahi recalled the incident. A fish mouth crack in a black oil pipeline had released fuel. By the time Pete and Keahi arrived, oil had entered Pearl Harbor estuary and heavily contaminated a nearby stream. The oil had washed up along the shoreline and onto the Navy's docks. Pete had gone with the Coasties in the Zodiac boat to determine the extent of the damage, and Keahi had stayed on shore to coordinate the disposal of oil-contaminated debris.

Keahi recalled that Pete had shone that day. He had enjoyed the response, lived for it. And now?

"That was a long time ago," Pete said, carefully placing other mementos into the box.

Then he pointed at two brown boxes on the bottom shelf of his bookcase. "Do you want my collection?" He pulled the smaller of the boxes off the shelf and let it drop two inches to the gray carpet. Keahi heard the sharp crack of glass against glass and wondered if something in the box had broken. He hoped not.

With the palm of his hand, Pete wiped off a layer of dust and bent back the box lid. He removed a glass vial from the box and held it up to the fluorescent ceiling light.

Keahi saw a black liquid floating on a clear, denser liquid. A thin layer of sediment rested on the bottom of the vial.

"Bunker C floating on salt water," Pete said.

Suddenly he shook the glass vial violently with a snapping motion of his wrist.

Again Pete held the vial overhead and they looked at it in the fluorescent light. The fuel oil and ocean water had mixed to form a new substance—a dark brown mousse. The water had disappeared into the oil, as cream disappears into milk to make homogenized milk.

Pete unscrewed the black cap and gently waved his fingers across the top of the vial in the direction of Keahi. "Want to smell it? No? It may look like chocolate mousse, but it smells like shit. Nothing worse than the smell of decaying Bunker C."

He recapped the glass vial and tossed it to Keahi, who caught it in his left hand, preventing it from shattering.

"Mix in a little sand, a few feathers, some seaweed and you know what you have?" Pete paused for effect and when Keahi didn't answer, he continued. "A turd. It's not something you'd like to see washing up onto the beaches in Waikiki."

"Eh, where did you get all these?"

"I've been collecting them for years. I have aviation gasoline and seawater from the airport. And diesel and seawater from a service station. Yeah, a variety of seawater cocktails."

Keahi noticed that each bottle was labeled with the date of collection, where the release had occurred, and the kind of petroleum.

"Do you want them?" Pete asked again.

"Thanks," Keahi said, grinning. "So I get to throw out your junks?"

"Well, you can throw *those* away, if you want. But I'd keep this one." Pete removed some cotton packing and held up a glass vial containing a black substance. "This is from the U.S.S. Arizona. It was collected underwater from the ship itself."

"How did you get that?"

Pete smiled.

Keahi carefully accepted the small vial and placed it in his breast pocket, respectfully. He had no doubt, whatsoever, that it was from the U.S.S. Arizona. Divers were always bringing up things from the ship; after all, it wasn't too long ago that someone had tried to sell a silver tea set from the ship.

They quickly packed three more beer boxes and stacked them in the hallway just outside Pete's cubicle.

"What are you going to do?" Keahi asked.

"I don't know."

"Those bruises look bad." Pete had yellow and purple bruises on both forearms.

"Yeah. I got no sleep last night. Every time I rolled onto my side, it was as if someone drove a pitchfork into my ribs. And every little noise woke me up. And I kept dreaming that I was lying on the floor in that hallway, with that heavy door on top of me, and I couldn't catch my breath. Then I'd wake up and be lying on my back in bed."

"Did you crack a rib?"

"No, but that lady doctor ran a battery of X-rays. She was thorough. I'd be in the hospital right now if she hadn't made the mistake of leaving me alone."

Keahi looked at Pete. His friend had refused treatment, which was a typical emergency responder, macho, maintain the image, bullshit kind of thing. *But that's who he is*, Keahi thought. *That's Pete.* He had friends who did the same thing after surfing accidents, friends who would rather convalesce on the beach than in a hospital room.

Together they carried the boxes to Pete's car and loaded them into the trunk and back seat. Actually, Keahi carried the boxes while Pete watched. Pete was in no condition to carry anything. In fact, Keahi wondered how Pete was going to steer.

"You know, this job isn't as fun as it used to be," Pete concluded. "I never imagined that we would be responding to an odor complaint and it would be a meth lab. That's for the DEA, not us. It ain't worth our lives, brah!"

They embraced in a gentle hug.

Then Pete climbed into his light blue Honda hatchback, waved *shaka* out the driver's window, grimaced in pain, and drove quickly away.

Keahi was left standing by himself in the parking lot.

On his way back to his work area, he passed Little Bill's cubicle. He stopped and surveyed it as he tried to make sense of everything that had happened. He had no doubt that he would be assigned either the playground investigation or the meth lab cleanup, now that Pete had quit. He mumbled, "What a mess." Suddenly he felt angry at Pete.

Little Bill's paperwork was strewn across his desk. "I suppose I will have to clean up your mess, too." Small piles of paper lay at strange angles on top of other small piles of paper, one pile on top of another pile, until the stack was so high it had cascaded sideways under its own disorganized weight, burying Little Bill's desk in an avalanche of white paper. Paper spilled out of Little Bill's mail tray, and more was crammed into every puka in his desk organizer. Paper was forced into every opening on his bookshelf. Paper was stuffed between emergency response equipment and laboratory catalogs.

Little Bill's right-hand desk drawer was open, the file cabinet was unlocked, and one file drawer was partly pulled out. Papers were higgledy-piggledy.

Keahi returned to his cubicle and sat in his kneeling posture chair at his desk and held his head in his hands. He felt numb.

He was aware of a tense atmosphere in the office, of people speaking quietly in small groups. After a few minutes, several dropped by his cubicle asking if Pete was okay, saying how awful it was about Little Bill. Keahi answered their questions, matched their concerned tones.

The director would be the one to speak to Bill's family. A memorial service would be planned. And there would be an investigation.

Keahi sighed.

He took his computer mouse in hand and surfed through OMER, his Obituary of Mitigated Emergency Responses. OMER was his personal database of emergencies that he had responded to over the years: a pesticide fire at a former sugar plantation, an oil spill into Pearl Harbor, a chlorine gas release at a hotel swimming pool, and dozens more, even burps—uncontrolled gas releases.

He leaned back in his chair and locked his fingers behind his head.

Burps.

Fumigants.

And now meth labs.

After a minute, he realized that he was staring at the phone, waiting for something to happen. Waiting for someone to call in the next release. He didn't like that. It was boring, yet stressful.

He had never enjoyed the adrenaline rush that always came with the initial call. In fact, waiting for the phone to ring was very stressful. Even now he was tense. Pete, however, enjoyed the rush. Pete had looked forward to the excitement of responding to an emergency, not knowing what he would discover. But Keahi never had enjoyed that. Even on the uneventful days, when there was no call, when there was no emergency to respond to, when nothing happened—he still left work tired and drained.

In fact, he hated his job, having been riffed into it by mistake—a mistake that had never been discovered and corrected, a typical bureaucratic error. Before the riff, he had worked in the Department of Business and Tourism's Office of Hawaiian Culture: specifically, the Cultural Affairs

Section. Keahi had happily arranged state-sponsored events for tourists such as the 'hula on the beach,' ukulele competitions at park venues, and authentic luaus.

But then he had received a letter from the director of his department informing him that his position as Music and Dance Coordinator was being eliminated and that they would attempt to place him in a different position. His RIF letter had read:

> "As provided by the reduction-in-force/layoff process, a department-wide search was conducted to identify a position for you. Regrettably, there were no bargaining unit positions or a position that you qualify for which is occupied by an incumbent who has fewer retention points than you.

> "Because you have at least 24 retention points, we have referred your name to the Employee Assessment and Adjustment Section (EAAS) to conduct a jurisdiction-wide search on your behalf. They will contact you directly on the outcome of the search."

This message was followed by the name of a person he could contact if he had any questions. And the letter had been signed 'sincerely' by the director.

About two months later he had received a second letter, placing him into a vacant position in a different department, the Department of Water, Wind and Sun, where he had remained until today. Needless to say, he was not qualified to be an Events Coordinator in an emergency response office. Nevertheless, he was placed into the position. And because the RIF process included no probation and no follow-up, he was promptly forgotten. Fortunately, Pete had taken him under his wing and had given him the necessary on-the-job training to survive.

Keahi often wondered who had made the mistake of placing him in his current position, but he never raised the question. After all, he needed the pay check and the health insurance. He had bills to pay. In fact, at the time of the RIF, he was already heavily in debt. Daniel's in-home care and treatment for Lou Gehrig's disease had been expensive, and Daniel only worked part-time jobs in the tourist industry. And besides, Daniel did not qualify under Keahi's health insurance because under Hawaii's law they were unable to marry. Consequently, the massive medical debt. Poor Daniel: diagnosed when he was 28, and dead before his thirtieth birthday.

The last thing Keahi wanted to do was to complain and lose his placement. Any job, given the poor economy, was better than no job. And the 21 days vacation, 21 days sick leave, and 14 holidays a year didn't suck, either. At least that is how he had reasoned it at the time.

He eased his conscience by telling Pete about the bureaucratic mistake. And what was Pete's reaction? He laughed it off and ordered Keahi a Level A personal protection suit, size XXXL, which Pete had to return because it was one size too large.

Unfortunately, the job did not match Keahi's artistic temperament. Waiting for the phone to ring drained him, and at the present moment, staring at the phone, his whole body was tense.

He thought about Little Bill's death, replaying the meth lab explosion in his mind, just as Pete had described it to him. He played the scene backwards and forwards, again and again, as if it were a movie. He had to learn from their mistakes.

He thought about Pete quitting. Keahi had lost not only his mentor but also his partner. Starting today, he would have to rely on less-experienced emergency responders; turnover at the department was terrible, and keeping qualified staff was impossible.

And he knew that without Pete, there was no buffer between himself and Santos. Not only was Santos an incompetent supervisor, he was also one of the dullest persons Keahi knew. Santos liked routine and disliked change. Unlike Pete, Santos was comfortable to sit in the office, to be nothing more than a career bureaucrat. Pete, on the other hand, liked novelty and disliked bureaucracy. Perhaps that's why Santos picked on him, because he knew that Pete had no respect for paper pushers. *But now that Pete's gone—and Little Bill, too—he's going to start picking on me.*

Suddenly feeling cornered, Keahi surveyed his cubicle. His desk organizer held several worn books: *Bryan's Sectional Map of Oahu*; *Guidebook for First Responders During the Initial Phase of a Hazardous Materials Incident*; *Guide to Hazardous Products around the Home*; a dictionary; and *Omeros*, a book of poetry.

What am I doing here?

He picked up a small paperweight off his desk, a hand-blown glass humpback whale, an anonymous gift from last year's Christmas gift exchange. Although the cost was not to exceed $10, he was sure that the little blue whale had cost considerably more. The fluted tail was delicate.

He set the blue whale down in front of the photo of Daniel, and a whole new set of emotions and memories came uninvited. Daniel was smiling in the picture, even though he had been battling Lou Gehrig's disease for more than a year when the photo was taken. Sometimes the photo cheered Keahi up, sometimes it depressed him. Today, Daniel's smile made Keahi feel sad and alone.

He slowly surveyed his cubicle. To the left of his desk were two old, black file cabinets and then a beige bookcase. A grass beach mat, loosely rolled up, leaned against the bookcase. An antique coat rack stood in the corner of the cubicle, within an easy arm's reach. Board shorts, a towel, and a T-shirt hung on the coat rack.

He suddenly recalled the cramped yeoman's office aboard the U.S.S. Bowfin. *Now that's a small work space!* He smiled.

Behind him, maps, tightly rolled up and wrapped with rubber bands, leaned against a cubicle wall beneath a white corkboard. The board was full of four-by-six photographs, pencil drawings, and scuffed-up field notes from a recent case: an abandoned black oil pipeline that ran along the coastline that had released thick, black oil.

Now that Pete had quit, Keahi was sure he would inherit all of Pete's cases, including the child care explosion case, so he cleared the corkboard and dropped all the photos, drawings and notes into his left-hand desk drawer.

Why have I stayed in this job?

He stood up and looked beyond the dull beige partitions

of his cubicle at the rest of the office. People were wandering around, undoubtedly talking about Little Bill's death, trying to find out what had happened. By now most of them had probably heard that Pete and Santos had argued and that Pete had quit. Keahi smiled. That disrespectful scene would become part of Pete's office folklore, just like his nickname, Picric.

Patrick Pete Petite had gotten his nickname after responding to a phone call from an old lady who had a bottle of picric acid – a highly shock-sensitive explosive – in her greenhouse. Her deceased husband, a chemistry professor, had brought the bottle home.

Keahi recalled Pete examining the bottle. The picric acid solution had evaporated, leaving behind yellow, shock-sensitive crystals. Picking up the bottle, unscrewing the lid, or just moving the bottle around could have caused it to explode. So Pete called the police, who called a military bomb demolition team. In the old lady's backyard, Keahi and Pete helped the bomb team dig a pit and shore it up with inch-and-a-half plywood boards. Then an experienced demolition expert, in full protective gear, moved the bottle of crystals to the pit and detonated it. Ever since that day, Keahi had called Pete Picric, or Pic for short.

While Keahi was thinking about that, his screensaver popped on; a prokaryotic cell floated to the center of the screen, where it started vibrating, slowly. Keahi watched the one-celled organism vibrate for five minutes. Life appeared in no hurry to go anywhere.

How did I get stuck in this job?

He answered himself: *Complacency.* It was easy to see

in hindsight. Complacency was a strong current that had swept him away and had drowned his talents.

After a while he put on his earphones, turned on his computer's CD player, and cranked up the volume on his favorite CD, "Facing Future." The majestic voice of Bruddah IZ—the late Hawaiian singer Israel Kamakawiwo'ole—began to soothe him, and he felt the tension leaving his shoulders.

He continued to watch the small cells as they vibrated slowly around the screen of his monitor. It was like watching computer-generated aquarium fish, but less colorful and with no computer-generated bubbles.

He thought about Liko and almost called him. Was he awake or was he sleeping in? Would he go to the beach or would he hang around the apartment pool?

At ten minutes to nine, after the CD ended, Keahi pulled off his earphones, rose from his kneeling posture chair, and stretched. Then he went to the break room, where he discovered that someone had brought *malasadas*—deep fried Portuguese donuts.

His friend Kwon Shin stood at the Mr. Coffee, filling his mug. He was thin, five-foot-five, with thinning black hair. He wore bright red suspenders, which held up a pair of loose-fitting Levis. The suspenders stretched loosely over his very narrow shoulders and a bright, silky aloha shirt. "Good ol' filter drip, coffee berry soup. I need my mid-morning fix."

"I had two cups of iced coffee at home," Keahi said. By the time he had arrived at work, after a half-hour trip through Waikiki, the caffeine had kicked in.

"Want another cup?"

"No, I don't drink coffee during the day. If the work doesn't keep me awake, I'd rather sleep till something happens." Keahi picked up a warm *malasada*. "I'll have a couple of these, though. They're *ono*." Usually he wouldn't eat the greasy, sugar-coated, deep-fried lumps of dough, but he was feeling dejected, and he had a tendency to eat sweets when his spirit was low.

"I heard about Little Bill," Kwon said, his voice soft.

"Yeah, it's hard to believe."

"He wasn't married, was he?"

"No, he was a bachelor, like us."

"Local family?"

"No, only relatives on the mainland."

"I heard that Pete quit."

"Yeah, and Santos took it personal."

"Of course. Santos is full of himself."

Keahi took another bite of the *malasada*. "You should have heard Pete tell him off, though. He said, 'I give respect where respect is due.'"

Kwon smiled. He resented all the managers. The suspenders, the loose-fitting blue jeans, the gaudy aloha shirts, they were all part of a carefully crafted, subtle attack on management. His aloha shirt today was a pattern of neon-colored bicycle helmets—all with long rear points.

"I'm going to miss Pete," Kwon said. "He always spoke his mind." Kwon stopped and sipped his coffee.

Keahi helped himself to another deep-brown *malasada*. "They're good when they're warm."

"How are *you* doing?" Kwon asked.

Surprised by the personal question, Keahi turned to face Kwon. "Okay, I guess. You know, I never had lunch with Little Bill. He wasn't here long enough for me to get to know him. That bothers me."

One of Keahi's strengths was relating to people. Missing the opportunity with Little Bill truly bothered him.

Keahi turned as Masako entered the break room in a simple black dress and casual red sandals, with thin leather straps. Keahi thought she looked stunning.

Masako said, "I heard about Little Bill on the ten o'clock news last night. That was terrible. They don't pay you guys enough to take those risks."

Masako walked across the room to the sink and started filling a plastic squeeze bottle from a gooseneck faucet. "I also heard about Pete. What are you guys going to do without him?"

Keahi wiped greasy sugar off his fingers onto a napkin and threw it into a trashcan. "I tried to change his mind."

The water overflowed the top of Masako's bottle and she screwed the cap on, tightly. "I don't know what I'd do if I was Pete."

Keahi shook his head. "He gave me an oil sample from the Arizona. Stop by and I'll show it to you."

"Has it been analyzed?" Masako asked.

"No, not yet."

"Split the sample with me, and I'll analyze it for you." She had a master's degree in chemical engineering and knew how to fingerprint fuels.

"Maybe ... I'll think about it."

There was a pause during which the three of them were quiet, and then Keahi ventured, "My nephew, Liko, is visiting. I took him to see the Arizona Memorial and the Bowfin yesterday."

Masako was interested. "The U.S.S. Bowfin?"

"Yeah."

Her eyes narrowed. "Did you know that the Bowfin sank a ship carrying more than 800 children?"

Kwon's arthritic hands almost dropped his coffee mug.

"Yeah." Masako pressed her lips together and nodded her head up and down, slowly. "The Tsushima Maru was an old ship. She was evacuating children from Okinawa when the Bowfin hit her with several torpedoes—broke her in half. She sank in minutes. Some of the children floated in rafts for days before a passing ship spotted them. A few children made it to a deserted island and were later rescued. But only a few survived."

Keahi and Kwon looked at each other.

"What?" Masako asked. "They omitted all that?"

"I don't know," Keahi said. "I don't remember seeing it."

He looked at Kwon. Kwon was staring at Masako.

"Have you been to the Peace Memorial Museum in Hiroshima?" Kwon asked.

"Of course," she said.

"I've also been there," Kwon said, reprovingly. "Nowhere in the exhibit do they mention the fact that Japan started the war with a surprise attack on Pearl Harbor. Don't you consider *that* a remarkable omission?"

Keahi's jaw dropped. Kwon's comment hung in the air like a foul odor. Masako covered her mouth in embarrassment in the traditional Japanese way and gave Kwon a condescending look. Then, without saying another word, she turned and walked out of the break room.

Kwon took a sip of coffee then asked, "Who was that?"

"Oh, I'm sorry," Keahi answered sarcastically. "I should have introduced you before you insulted her. Her name is Masako. She works in the Hazardous Waste Unit."

"Did you see her nails?"

"Her fingernails?"

"They were manicured. Can you believe that?"

He gave Kwon a quizzical look, puzzled that Kwon had even noticed her fingernails. He wondered what difference it made if Masako's fingernails were manicured. In fact, he liked to have his own nails manicured once in a while.

"Are you going swimming today?" Kwon asked.

"Yeah."

"At lunchtime?"

"Yeah, at noon."

Kwon set his mug on the counter and, grasping the handle of the coffeepot in both hands, carefully refilled his mug. "I'll see you at lunch," he said, returning the pot to the Mr. Coffee. Then he left the break room, cradling the warm mug of coffee in his arthritis-ravaged hands.

Alone, Keahi carefully wrapped up two *malasadas* in paper towels, saying to himself, "For later, after lunch." One advantage of weight lifting was being able to eat sweets whenever he wanted. The calories literally evaporated during his grueling workouts.

He returned to his cubicle. Eukaryotic cells were now floating across his computer screen. In evolutionary time, it had taken the eukaryotic cells two billion years to evolve from their ancestors, the prokaryotic cells. But on his computer's screensaver, it had taken only two hours.

Keahi's thoughts floated from the eukaryotes to Little Bill. *Little Bill walks into a meth lab and gets his insides jellied.*

"Damn!"

Didn't Little Bill smell something? Suspect something? That's the most important part of our job: to identify the hazards, to protect ourselves.

And why did Little Bill enter first? Pete was senior. He had the experience.

Keahi sighed.

Maybe Pete screwed up and knew it. Maybe that's why he quit so suddenly.

And what's wrong with Kwon? Why so rude?

At lunchtime, Keahi and Kwon rode in Kwon's beater, an old Kia, down a side street from their office to Ala Moana Boulevard, then three minutes to a shaded parking space along a street fronting the Ala Moana Beach Park.

Using their car doors as a screen, they changed their clothes with a *lava lava*—a large, colorful beach towel—wrapped around their waists: they stripped off their jeans and pulled on their swimsuits. Kwon neatly folded his red suspenders, jeans and old aloha shirt, and laid them carefully on the driver's seat.

"Be careful not to wrinkle that gaudy shirt," Keahi said sarcastically. "We don't want you looking frumpy. That might piss off management. We wouldn't want that, would we?"

Kwon smiled as they locked up the car and started walking across the asphalt parking lot in the direction of the beach. "What do you know about Masako?"

"She looks great in black."

Kwon frowned. "But what do you know about her?"

"Her father has money." Several steps later Keahi added, "He owns a successful marriage business. Several marriage chapels."

"I bet"—Kwon's voice was bitter and biting—"I bet he hires only Japanese nationals and Japanese-Americans."

"What?" Keahi frowned, taken aback. "Where in the world did *that* come from?" He glanced at Kwon walking beside him. Kwon's body was wiry and coiled, tense like a spring.

"I didn't like her comment about the Bowfin—her attitude."

"So?" They stepped onto a sidewalk that led to the beach. "What does that have to do with her father and his marriage business?"

"Nothing, but I've seen it before."

"Seen what?"

"She thinks that she's better than us."

"You could tell that by one comment she made about the Bowfin? Or did I miss something else? Oh yes, her fingernails. They were pretentious, weren't they?"

"I've seen it before," Kwon said.

Keahi glanced at Kwon. *Why is he so bitter?*

Reaching the end of the sidewalk, they stepped out of their slippers and carried them as they strolled across hot white sand to a spot near two girls who were lying on green beach towels, basking in thongs in the unforgiving sun. Keahi quickly worked his feet beneath the hot surface into cooler sand. Then he set down his slippers, side-by-side. He removed his sunglasses and rolled them up in his *lava lava*, which he placed on top of the slippers.

Then he stretched: first his arms, next his shoulders, then his chest, and last his back muscles. Then he executed three deep knee squats.

He felt the sun's energy burning his shoulders. "Where are the trades?"

"Where's the ozone?"

"What?"

"We got a tip, actually an anonymous complaint, about Freon smugglers."

My god, Keahi thought. *What do YOU know about smugglers? Or Freon?* He joked, "I thought you clean air guys issued permits, pushed paper—exciting stuff li' dat."

Kwon ignored him. "A building superintendent bought some bootlegged Freon—*poli 'ahu*—for his hotel's old central air conditioning. That's what they call it on the street—*poli 'ahu*, the snow goddess. He was making a killing until the high moisture and the impurities in the Freon crashed his chiller." Kwon grinned. "He had to call in a repairman. One thing led to another and finally we got a tip.

"Now everybody is involved—the EPA, the Customs Service, the IRS, and even the FBI. They're calling it Operation Icy Wind."

"You're kidding, right?"

"Hell no! They smuggled it in 150-pound cylinders disguised as helium. And then sold it for more than a thousand dollars a cylinder."

Keahi whistled.

"You know," Kwon said, "I have to take Plaquenil for my rheumatoid arthritis, and it makes me very sensitive to the sun and sunburn."

"Well, I hope you hang' em by their balls." Keahi quickly glanced sideways at the sunbathing girls, hoping they hadn't heard his comment. They didn't appear to be listening.

He walked to the water's edge and dangled a foot into the ocean. "Ah! Chilly!" He shivered, clattering his teeth for dramatic effect.

"Not really," Kwon said. "The ocean is 75 degrees this time of year. But it will warm up to 83 degrees by August."

Keahi glanced at Kwon. He was an exceptional repository of data. In fact, collecting and recalling information was one of his strengths. In contrast, Keahi had no idea what the water temperature was. He only knew that it was cooler this time of year—for him, almost too cool.

They waded in until they were waist deep and then Keahi rolled over onto his back and wet his hair. He gazed skyward for a few seconds, gauged the intensity of the sun—it was brutal!—then stood up on his feet to put on his swim mask. Chunks of coral rock jabbed into his soles and he struggled to maintain his balance; he didn't want to stumble around on the annoying skeletal rock.

Kwon dove, quick and shallow, to wet his hair. A deeper

dive would have been dangerous because, although the sandy bottom dropped off quickly to twenty feet, the water was murky and it was hard to judge where the sandy ledge ended and the deep channel began. Kwon surfaced, and as soon as he donned his orange goggles—the ones with large silicon eye cups—he was swimming parallel to the beach in the deep swimming channel, which had originally been dredged for boats.

Keahi floated out a few yards on his stomach then did a breaststroke, leisurely, until his body acclimated to the cool water. After that he started the American crawl, slowly, then gradually picked up speed until he was stroking a steady quarter time count, breathing every other stroke, racing through the water.

He swam to a white pole in the middle of the channel, far down the beach, then back again. His speed depended on the currents, the wind, and his state of mind. Today the water was fast.

As usual, Kwon beat him back, but he had swum only a fraction as far. In short distances Kwon was faster because he was skinny and lacked the muscle mass that Keahi dragged through the water. Keahi guessed that Kwon couldn't swim long distances, probably because of his damaged elbow joint; even swimming short distances must be painful.

Kwon was now floating on his back, the sun shining on his face and hairy chest. "Did you know that the earth is 93 million miles from the sun?"

"No," Keahi said.

"And did you know that we are moving 67,000 miles per hour?"

"Really?"

They left the water, gathered up their *lava lavas* and slippers, and went directly to the beachside shower, where they washed the sea salt off their bodies so they wouldn't feel sticky. They toweled off and strolled back to Kwon's old car, dressed, and combed their hair using the car mirrors. Kwon sped back to the office, car windows down, the wind blowing their hair dry. The entire outing took less than an hour, including thirty minutes of swim time.

The swim usually helped Keahi to relax.

"You know," Kwon said, "that Masako is a real bitch. The more I think about her, the angrier I get." His misshapen hands tightly gripped the steering wheel: one positioned at 3 o'clock, the other, 9 o'clock.

So much for stress reduction, Keahi thought.

Back in his cubicle, Keahi stared at his screensaver; multi-cellular organisms had replaced the eukaryotic cells. Toi, his coworker and friend who gave him the screensaver, had told him that eukaryotic cells had taken a billion years to evolve into complex multi-cellular organisms. Keahi tried to put a billion years into perspective; he recalled that Kwon had told him the island of Oahu had existed for little more than 2 million years. What was the difference between a billion years and 2 million years? How could he fathom the difference when he was only in his fifties?

Ten fingers, two eyes and one nose!

A billion was incomprehensible.

He put his earphones on, turned on Bruddah Iz, and watched the multi-cellular organisms for half an hour. They ate, grew, repaired themselves, reproduced, wandered around, and then died.

His phone rang—two short rings, which meant it was an internal call. He picked it up, relieved that it wasn't an emergency response call. "Keahi here."

"Finish Pete's case." Santos cleared his throat. "Write it up and file it. I want it wrapped up. Today. The file is in your mailbox."

"If I—"

But before Keahi could finish his sentence, Santos hung up; Santos rarely left an opportunity for questions.

Keahi sullenly walked to the mail table and pulled the brown file from his mailbox. He returned to his cubicle. He put away Bruddah IZ and put on Bach's *Goldberg Variations*. He then spent the next two hours reading and studying the file, reviewing Pete's notes.

I should have been helping Pete with this, instead of sightseeing with Liko.

He studied a hand-drawn map Pete had made. Something about the map bothered him.

He telephoned Kwon. "Napoleon assigned me Kehena Kare. Can you give me a hand?"

"Why? What's wrong?"

"There's no smoking gun."

"I'd like to, but I'm busy with my Freon case. I need to go to the courthouse, search through the property records, and identify the owners of the warehouse where the canisters of Freon were illegally stored. I'll be tied up for days."

"Kwon, that's the Stone Age way. I have a software program that will bring you into the twenty-first century. It's one of my secret weapons."

"Secret weapon?" Kwon laughed into the phone. "Why do you emergency guys get all the toys?"

"Because it's a gift from the EPA. We use the software to investigate bad actors, persons who contaminate the *aina*. I can look up their assets—real estate, yachts, cars, home values—and determine if a bad actor has the money to clean up a polluted site. It's a powerful program." Keahi paused for effect. "Help me with the playground explosion and I'll let you use the software. It will save you a lot of time."

"You have a deal," Kwon said, without hesitating. "I still need to make a run to the courthouse, though."

"Why?"

"Because I need to know who the owner of the property is before I can check his assets, right? I'll stop by your cubicle after four."

"I won't be here," Keahi said. "I've got to leave early. I'll leave the software CD and manual in the top drawer of my file cabinet." Keahi smiled; he knew that Kwon would like the new toy.

"Thanks."

"You'll be surprised at the information available from public records. And this software puts it at your fingertips. It's powerful."

Keahi felt relieved that Kwon had agreed to help. No one was better at interpreting field data and statistics. He had a knack for models and numbers, a talent that Keahi didn't have.

He pinned Pete's hand-drawn map to the corkboard. The sketch, drawn to scale, showed the location of playground equipment. A large "X" was marked over a swing set and labeled in capital letters, "AREA OF FIRE."

There was no smoking gun—no reason for a fire.

Keahi took the back benchseat in TheBus; work had just ended and he was going to the gym. It was a hard plastic seat and he could feel the heat radiating from the large diesel engine directly behind him, on the other side of the metal wall, but he needed the extra legroom. He sat in the middle of the seat and stretched out his long legs into the aisle. When the back doors opened to let passengers off, Keahi could smell the exhaust from all the cars near gridlock on the boulevard. It left a metallic taste in his mouth.

He revisited the clandestine lab explosion and Little Bill's death. It puzzled him. *Why hadn't Pete recognized the signs of danger: cigarette butts discarded just outside the apartment door, the smell of starter fluid, the stench of acetone?* The police or the DEA, wearing ballistic protection equipment and fire retardant clothing, should have made the initial entry. Little Bill could have been shot. Actually, that was more likely than an explosion.

Suddenly Keahi felt angry at Pete for quitting and leaving him without any answers. And he also felt abandoned—by Pete, Little Bill and even Kwon, who was behaving strangely. *Why was Kwon obsessed with Masako?* He didn't even know her. His behavior was disconcerting, and his comment about the Hiroshima memorial was shamefully tasteless.

He was seeing a side of Kwon that he didn't like. How well did he really know him, anyway?

As Keahi surveyed the overcrowded bus, he recalled another statistic that Kwon had recently shared with him: the world's population was quickly approaching seven billion people, with more than one million of them here on Oahu. So why did he feel abandoned and isolated, as if he were on an island by himself? *More than six billion people in the world and I am on a crowded bus and I am lonely!*

Sitting up the aisle were two young boys. He had no choice but to look in their direction, at their scuffed shoes, ragged T-shirts and all but worn-out skateboards.

They were seated across from a young girl whose appearance screamed "Look at me, I'm a lesbian."

The boys found the girl irresistible and started teasing her, making fun of her pale, Goth appearance.

Several older Filipino-Americans scattered throughout the bus sat and listened passively as the boys shot rude, derogatory comments at the girl. Keahi thought that the Filipino-Americans looked tired. They were probably going home after a hard day of physical work, or perhaps they were on their way to a second or even a third job.

The punks, finding themselves unchecked, unleashed a vicious barrage of criticism against the girl.

Finally . . . tears.

At that moment, two elderly Canadian tourists spoke up. "Stop it!" the man ordered. "Leave her alone!" the woman added.

"Where did you get those blue legs?" one of the punks yelled back, making fun of the Canadians' bright, sun-starved, blue-white legs.

Should I do something? Keahi asked himself. But he didn't want to aggravate the situation, hurt anyone, or be hurt.

He looked out the bus windows. They were covered with a sun-reflecting material, which made the window glass look like it was melting.

Why do some people find satisfaction in bullying others?

At the next bus stop, the Canadians fled through the back bus door and into the International Market Place with a terrified look in their eyes. Keahi doubted that it was their intended stop.

Three stops later Keahi got off the bus too, but on Kuhio Avenue, two blocks *mauka*—on the mountain side—of the gym.

As the bus pulled away from the curb he saw the punks take seats on both sides of the girl. Most of the Filipino-Americans had gotten off and were now walking down the street to their tiny apartments in the high rises scattered throughout the heart of Waikiki, or to their next job.

A few more stops and the driver would be at his rest stop, in front of the Kapiolani Band Stand. Keahi had waited at that stop not long ago. He guessed that the driver would get off the bus, go to the restroom, have a cigarette. The girl would be alone with the punks.

But it's a busy area, Keahi thought. *That area of Kapiolani Park is a busy area, lots of people coming and going.*

She could get off the bus if she needed to.

Firmly gripping three hundred pounds of weight with both hands, Keahi moved underneath the padded section of the bar and aligned it on his shoulders. Then, with an upward motion, he raised it off the upright rack, transferring the dead weight to his legs. He took two steps backwards, cautiously. Then, after carefully adjusting his stance—feet parallel, toes pointed slightly outward, ankles shoulder-width apart—he slowly let his knees bend until his thighs made a ninety-degree angle with the floor. Then he pushed upward with his quadriceps, exhaling and grunting, exerting maximum physical effort. And then he performed five more leg squats.

After that he paused at the top to catch his breath.

"One more," he told Angelica and Carol, breathing loudly. They were standing on each side of the barbell. His massive chest swelled.

As he lowered his glutes towards the floor, his leg muscles failed. Instantly, Carol and Angelica spotted him and kept the weights from crushing him against the floor. They helped him stand up, shaking and wobbling. Together they returned the bar to the upright rack.

He felt ashamed, suddenly, because their help made him realize how badly he had failed to stand up for the girl on the bus. *I deserve to be squashed against the floor like a bug,* he thought. *If Carol and Angelica knew that I did nothing . . . .*

He looked at them. They were beautiful, Carol with her shiny black hair and silver braces, Angelica with her long blond hair and green eyes. Both had strong bodies. Carol was bulked up, Angelica svelte like a marathon runner.

"Is the snorkeling still on for Hanauma Bay?" Angelica asked Keahi.

"Sure," he said, still breathing deep and exhaling loudly. "We're looking forward to it."

"Good, it's about time we met your nephew," Carol said, her voice a bit testy.

Later, after the workout, when they met on the sidewalk in front of the gym, the women gave Keahi a present wrapped in yellow tissue paper, in a white sack with rope handles. He unwrapped it and read the title: *Island Barbecues, Hawaiian-style.*

"Thanks," he said, very pleased with the gift yet puzzled. "What's the occasion?"

"We found it on a sales table at Macy's under a 'Father's Day' sign," Carol answered, grinning.

That made Keahi chuckle. He'd scored an unexpected Father's Day present. His first.

"Well, thank you, both of you, very much. Looks like barbecue this weekend, after we snorkel. And that reminds me Angelica, thanks for the brok da mouf stew. Liko liked it."

Then they asked him to go to Hula's Bar later in the evening. He knew they were just being polite, but he was still feeling guilty about not defending the girl on TheBus so he surprised them, and himself, and agreed to go.

Keahi's walk home from the gym took him past the entrance to the zoo and the statue of Gandhi. He approached the statue as a student would approach his guru, with a mix of respect and awe. The bronze Mahatma was frozen in mid-stride atop a four-foot pedestal, firmly gripping his bamboo walking cane. Gandhi was dressed in homespun cotton cloth and well-worn sandals. He gazed through Ben Franklin-style wire-rimmed spectacles towards the ocean.

Many years ago, Keahi had seen the movie *Gandhi*. It had made a deep, lasting impression on him. Afterwards, he had read everything he could find about Gandhi and studied his teachings. Moreover, he had adopted some of Gandhi's beliefs as his own, especially Gandhi's philosophy regarding non-violence. Over the years he had grown to revere the loving-kindness, simplicity, and humility of the man.

"My troubles seem so big, so important, Babu. But now, just being here with you makes me feel so much better."

Keahi imagined that Gandhi replied: "Come with me. Walk with me to the ocean. You see, I am almost there."

"Why are you walking to the ocean?" Keahi asked.

"Because like yours, my troubles seem so big, so important. But once we reach the ocean, our problems will float away."

Keahi lamented the fact that he had no living role model other than Picric, but that was work-related. Gandhi, on the other hand, left him awestruck. He exemplified the leadership qualities Keahi respected: quiet strength and courage and determination. A frail man marching against formidable forces.

Whenever Keahi stood before the statue, things snapped into focus. His perception of himself and the world realigned and took their proper perspective. His thoughts calmed down and he was able to focus on what was truly important.

What could he do about the clandestine lab and the explosion and the death of Little Bill? Nothing. What could he do about the increase of theft in Hawaii, and Liko's stolen luggage? Nothing. What could he have done about the Japanese tourist knocked down in Waikiki by the thief? The punks on the bus? Yes, he should have done something in those cases.

"I should have grabbed the purse-snatcher and held him for the police. But what if I had injured him?"

This time Gandhi didn't answer.

"And I should have spoken up on the bus, taken a seat next to the girl."

"Yes," Gandhi agreed, "non-violence does not mean non-action."

"But what can I do about the playground explosion?"

"Prevent another explosion," Gandhi suggested.

Keahi smiled.

Liko and Keahi ate the last of Angelica's stew as they watched the evening sun set from the lanai. It was a cloud shadow sunset. Another workday was ending.

"How was your day, Liko?" Keahi spread some mango chutney on a slice of white bread.

Liko dipped a celery stalk in a kukui nut relish.

"Some local kids stole my Warrior Gyms." Liko took a sip of red wine. "At first they thought I was local, too. One asked, 'What school you went?' I told 'em I went to high school in Nevada, and they acted like I'd dropped to earth from the moon."

"When I got back from my swim, my Warrior Gyms were stolen." Liko stabbed the relish with another celery stalk. It was too salty.

"I suppose you left them lying on top of your towel?" Keahi asked.

Liko didn't answer. *When I see those guys again, I'm going to kick their asses.*

They finished dinner and set their empty bowls in the sink, and then Keahi started a DVD of the six o'clock news. He always recorded the evening news, both six and ten o'clock. He stood in front of the television as he fast-forwarded, looking for information about the meth lab explosion or the playground explosion, but found nothing, so he clicked the player off.

"I've been assigned the lead on the playground explosion."

Impressed, Liko said, "I wish I had a job like yours."

Keahi studied him for a moment. *He has no idea how much I dislike my job. I should have been a performer or a Music and Dance Coordinator. Definitely not an emergency responder!* He shook his head.

"I won't have as much time to spend with you."

"That's okay."

"I'll need the car, too, so you'll have to ride TheBus."

Keahi fished the cookbook out of his backpack, and then they went back out onto the lanai and settled into the blue-striped lounge chairs. Keahi handed the cookbook to Liko. "Why don't you pick out our first barbecue?"

Liko thumbed through it. "Eh, this is a nice book. I've always wanted to barbecue. Not just cook hamburgers and steaks, but really barbecue." He added, "I worked at a steak house, you know?"

"See any recipes for ribs?" Keahi suggested.

Liko read aloud, "A'u. How about barbecued a'u?"

"Swordfish?"

"Is that what a'u is?"

"Yeah, let's try that one."

They listened to a hidden gecko barking in the twilight.

"Did you know that we are 93 million miles from the sun?" Keahi said, admiring the dim, twilight rays of the setting sun.

"Yeah?" Liko gave Keahi a glance and decided he was being serious. "That's pretty far, I guess."

Keahi produced a small vial from his shirt pocket and handed it to Liko. "You'll never guess what this is."

"You changed the oil in your car?"

Keahi chuckled.

Liko flinched. The chuckle reminded him of his mother, the way she laughed.

"No," Keahi said. "It's from the U.S.S. Arizona. It's a sample of the fuel oil leaking from the battleship."

Liko's fingers closed around the bottle and his knuckles turned white. If he had squeezed just a little harder the glass would have cracked in the palm of his hand.

After a short walk across Kapiolani Park to Kalakaua Avenue and Kapahulu Street, Keahi met Angelica and Carol at Hula's Bar. He found them at a table next to a window overlooking the ocean. The gentle trade winds caressed them.

"How's your nephew?" Carol asked.

"Some local kids stole his sunglasses. At San Souci. He went for a swim and when he got back his glasses were gone."

It was *pau hana* Friday, so Keahi bought a two-dollar beer for himself, a gin and tonic for Carol, and a ginger ale for Angelica.

What a beautiful couple, he thought.

When they had first met as teenagers under the old banyan tree at the original Hula's Bar on Kuhio Avenue, Keahi had immediately been attracted to their warmth, their affection for each other, and their friendliness. Since then, the three of them had lifted weights together several times a week and now they had a deep, strong friendship.

He looked around the bar. Several men were playing pool, dancing, or like him, quietly having drinks and conversations with old friends.

"Are we feeling *kolohe* tonight?" Carol asked Keahi.

"No, no mischief tonight," Keahi replied. "I'm too tired to be naughty." There was a hint of laughter in his response. "I wish Daniel was here."

"Now, don't get weepy on me," Carol said.

"My dear, dear Carol," Keahi said, "do you know that we are 93 million miles from the sun?"

"What a lonely thought!" Angelica interjected.

Keahi nodded agreement.

She leaned across the table and took off his sunglasses, held them up to the light, and frowned disapprovingly. She handed them to Carol, who dunked a paper napkin in a glass of ice water and then slowly, carefully cleaned the lenses. Then Carol passed the glasses back to Angelica, who held them up to the light and peered through them again. "Mo' bettah, my dear friend. You need someone to take care of you." She handed the glasses back to him.

"Yes, I suppose I do," he said. "I don't want to grow old alone."

"When I first met Daniel he was wearing thick plastic glasses." Keahi paused for effect. "And a perfectly ghastly aloha shirt, and matching aloha shorts! *All* his clothes were tacky. Just dreadful. Altogether dreadful!"

"Yes, you've told us," Carol said. "You had to take him in hand and show him how to dress, to style his hair, to—"

Keahi felt Angelica's foot brush against his leg as she kicked Carol under the table.

Carol winced.

I'm talking like an old gay widow. For a moment he wondered: *Is that what I'm becoming? A bitter, old widow?*

Then he looked around the room at the young, available men. Contrary to popular opinion, he knew that young gay men were not very interested in older men like him, despite his phenomenal body. They were interested in kids their own age, naturally. And these young men were no different.

He did notice a handsome older man seated at a nearby table, though.

"Is love an illusion?" he asked.

"Heavens no."

"Are you enjoying Liko's visit?"

"I guess so."

"You'd make a great father," Angelica said teasingly.

"Huh?"

"Have you ever thought of having children?" she fired, point blank. Her green eyes focused steadily on Keahi as she waited for his reply.

Keahi didn't know what to say to that. After a long pause he said, "Right. I'll pencil that into my social calendar: have children. Step one, figure out how." He chuckled, conscious that Angelica's gaze was fastened on his face.

I guess she likes my chuckle.

CHAPTER SIX

AT TWO O'CLOCK, THE HOTTEST TIME of the Hawaiian day, Keahi knocked on the front door of his auntie's Black Point Beach home. She lived in an exclusive gated community just around the corner from Diamond Head Beach, nestled away among royal palms. Liko, standing next to Keahi, listened to the rustle of the palm fronds. The trade winds were blowing side shore instead of the traditional east-northeast.

"Aloha!" Auntie opened her front door—a massive Koa door—and gave Keahi a warm, motherly hug. He patted her gently on the back and leaned down to kiss her affectionately on both tanned cheeks.

Her pungent pikake perfume almost overpowered him. He knew it was her favorite, but she was wearing it strong, which he dismissed as a mistake of her old age. He guessed she was in her eighties.

"You look great, Auntie." She was short and slender,

about 125 pounds, and had her hair in loose braids coiled like a crown.

She smiled, relishing the compliment. Then she saw Liko.

"Liko? How wonderful to see you!" She hugged him, pulling him down to her small frame. She had tremendous strength in her hands and arms for an elderly lady.

Liko embraced her and kissed her on both cheeks, as he had just seen Keahi kiss her. The ritual, however, left him embarrassed.

She escorted them into her grand home and seated them in orange leather chairs in her living room, which reminded Liko of a room in a museum. The room was filled with items on display: many were behind glass cabinet doors, or underneath inverted, glass domes on tables, or inside glass-covered picture boxes hung on the wall.

"Would you like plantation iced tea?" she asked.

"Yes," they replied in unison.

"Good! I'm thirsty too. I have a pitcher in the kitchen. I'll be right back."

Before either Keahi or Liko could offer to help, she left the room.

"What a strong grip!" Liko commented.

"She's happy to see you."

Liko stood up, meandered around, took in the displays. "Is this where you got your musical instruments?"

"Yes, I borrowed them from Auntie's collection."

"Are they antiques, too?"

"Yes, they are."

"Even the nose flute?"

"Yes."

Liko opened a display cabinet and picked up an oil-polished bowl made of red koa. He turned it over in his hands, admiring its three cores of heartwood. As he set it back on the glass shelf, it slipped and struck the thick glass, making a loud thud. "Everything's on glass and behind glass—I guess she doesn't like people touching her stuff."

"That's to protect it from the salt air. She doesn't mind if you pick them up. I've dusted and waxed and cleaned everything in here, many times." Keahi smiled at Liko. In fact, he had spent hours polishing and studying the antiques, happily.

Liko carefully closed the display case.

The next moment, Auntie returned holding a silver tray—solid silver, Liko guessed—on which set a Waterford crystal pitcher filled with iced tea, three empty crystal tea glasses, silver teaspoons, and a large crystal sugar bowl. The tendons stood out on her tanned hands as she carried the tray to Liko, who was still standing by the display case. He lightened her load by one glass of Tahitian iced tea and a napkin. Keahi also took a glass.

"It's already sweetened, but if you like it sweeter help yourself to the sugar."

Liko took a sip. "No, this is fine," he said. "It's good. Thank you."

She set the tray down on the coffee table and then turned to squarely face Liko.

"Feel the weight of that golden *umeke*," Auntie said, nodding her head in the direction of a wooden bowl behind a glass cabinet to the right of Liko.

Liko set his glass of tea down on the coffee table and stepped back to the glass cabinet, opened it, and picked up the *umeke*. It was a wider bowl than the one he had just dropped, and it had a thinner lip. "Yes, it's a heavy, solid bowl." He set it down on the glass shelf, gently.

"If I remember correctly, it was made from a tree crotch." She glanced over her shoulder, caught Keahi's eyes, and winked.

He smiled at her subtle joke.

"Now, pick up that bowl on the shelf above it."

Liko obeyed. "It's much lighter!"

Its dull, light brown surface was decorated with primitive, geometric designs.

"That is an *umeke pohue*. It's made from a wild gourd. That one was used to serve *poi*. Do you like *poi*?"

"I dunno," Liko answered. "I haven't tried it." He looked at Keahi. "I keep hearing about it, though."

He set the bowl down, and as he closed the cabinet, he thought, *So this is my Hawaiian culture? Wooden bowls and gourds? Purple, gooey foods?* "Where did you get all this stuff?"

"Collecting Hawaiian artifacts was one of Joe's passions," Auntie said. "If Joe were here, he could tell you the history of each piece."

"Joe?"

"My late husband, Joe. You would have liked him. Everyone liked him. But he died before you were born."

Liko felt embarrassed; he knew as much about his relatives as he knew about his Hawaiian heritage, which was nothing. His mother's trailer outside Las Vegas was a long way from Hawaii.

"Auntie, tell Liko how you and Joe met," Keahi suggested.

She smiled. "Let's sit down first."

Liko took her arm and walked her the few feet to one of the orange chairs; she didn't need any assistance, so it was mostly a gesture of respect. He sat down in the chair adjacent to her.

She began her story. "I was a freelance writer on assignment in Kalapapa." She looked carefully at Liko's face for a sign of recognition. "Kalapapa?"

His face was blank.

"The leper colony on the island of Molokai?"

She added, "Liko, do you know who Father Damien was?"

Liko shook his head no.

"The saint who devoted his life to working with the lepers?"

"No."

"Why Liko!" she said, exasperated, "You don't know *anything.*"

Liko didn't take the rebuke personally. He knew it was meant to shame him into being more interested in his heritage. His mother had occasionally tried the same tactic, also without effect.

"Well, well. Back to my story. I went to Kalapapa hoping to find a human interest story. Instead I found Joe, living at the compound and researching medicines."

"He was a doctor?" Liko asked.

"Yes, but he never had his own practice. He was what you would call a research doctor—a pharmaceutical researcher. I fell madly in love with him.

"After Kalapapa, I followed him to the mainland where he completed his research on a new medicine for leprosy. Then we moved to California where he oversaw clinical trials for a mainland, pharmaceutical company.

"We bought the property here at Blackpoint Beach shortly after we returned to Hawaii. That was many years ago."

"He must have made a lot of money." Liko waved his arms across the room in front of him, highlighting the expensive real estate and museum quality furnishings and antiques on display.

"His research was original and led to several pharmaceutical patents. Yes, it made us rich." Auntie smiled at Liko. "And houses were cheaper then, not at all like today. Money went a lot farther in those days."

"Did you write your story about the lepers?"

"Oh yes, the story was about Joe. It was the first really good human interest story I wrote."

Again, Liko was embarrassed. *Joe was a leper? I should have known that. Why didn't Mom tell me?*

"I stopped writing after he died. I lost interest. For a long time I didn't care about anything. I even quit the newspaper business."

"Tell him about your Bumbye cartoon," Keahi said, encouraging her.

"Like I said, after Joe died I quit the paper. But I needed a hobby, something to occupy my mind. So I began drawing. It was wonderful therapy! I wasn't very good, but I had a talent for simple drawings.

"Well, one day something in the local news riled me. You know how every once in a while you read something in the local paper that makes you mad? And not just mad, but furious? Well, I read something that really upset me so I drew a cartoon, a simple characterization of a local senator. I added a satirical caption and mailed it to the editor. The editor and I were good friends, you see, so he published the cartoon.

"Neither of us expected the favorable response it received! The editor called and asked me to do another one! And that's how my local cartoon, Senator Bumbye was born."

"And that's how she made her second fortune," Keahi added, smiling. "For a while Bumbye was everywhere—on T-shirts, bumper stickers, even on surf boards."

Liko now noticed that one wall of the room was decorated with a series of framed cartoons and original artwork, including a collage of Bumbye memorabilia tastefully arranged inside a heavy Koa shadow box.

"How's your mother?" Auntie asked.

Liko thought about his mother dancing her drunken hula. "She gets by."

"Liko, I want you and I to get to know each other."

Liko couldn't imagine why she would want that.

"Did you know that Keahi came to live with me? And when he was younger than you!" Auntie's voice sounded happy, pleased, and satisfied in the moment.

"She means she kept me off the street," Keahi said. "When I was in the eighth grade I ran away from home. I lived on the streets until Auntie found me and asked me to live with her." *She provided me a tolerant environment to grow up in,* he thought.

"This lady," Keahi nodded towards his aunt, "she is the kindest lady you will ever know."

Auntie beamed, her face glowing. And then she chuckled, too.

There's that chuckle again, Liko noted. *My mom's chuckle. Keahi has it, my aunt has it. Must be a family trait.*

Keahi wondered if he should tell Liko about his gay friends. Deciding to explore the risk, he ventured: "Liko, many of my friends have had a much harder time of it than me. When my friend Carol told her parents she was a lesbian, her stepfather ordered her out of their house. He feared she would be a bad influence on her younger sister. Carol's mother sided with the stepfather and Carol suddenly found herself without a family and without a home. She was fifteen and living on the beach. It wasn't long after that that I met her and Angelica outside Hula's Bar. She lived here for a while."

"I found her in one of my guest rooms one morning," Auntie said, still chuckling. "What a surprise! Keahi had sneaked her into the house. She was a skinny, scared kid."

"Auntie's home has always been a place of refuge," Keahi told Liko. Keahi wanted to say, "Here, I was gay—period. I could just be myself." But he didn't. Instead he studied Liko, fearful that too much had already been said, fearful that Liko would react negatively. He noted that Liko was listening, yet he was also keeping silent.

Auntie sipped her tea, her kind eyes peering over the lip of the crystal tea glass. "And I bought Keahi his first set of weights," she proclaimed proudly.

"I still remember how proud Keahi was when he started those weights. He helped Carol start, too. They spent many hours here lifting weights together. Before that, she was scrawny and her black hair was tangled and she wore dirty clothes. She had no self-esteem."

"No self-esteem?" Keahi asked. "You're thinking of Angelica,

Auntie. Carol may have looked grungy, but she never lost confidence in *who* she was. That's why her stepfather kicked her out."

"Maybe," Auntie conceded. "Now Angelica—she was a wild kitten!"

"She would scratch you as soon as look at you," Keahi said to Liko, agreeing with his aunt. *And she is manic depressive and probably an alcoholic. But no need to mention that.* "But now she's a strong, beautiful woman."

"Those were great times, Auntie—chants, hula, pumping up." Keahi almost added: *It was intoxicating, exhilarating.*

"Shall we go to the backyard lanai?" she suggested.

"Yes, that would be nice," Keahi replied.

As they left the 'museum room,' Auntie started a CD, and Keahi recognized his own voice recorded at the Hoku-alihi Festival competition. He was chanting in Hawaiian.

They walked across designer floor tiles and large, plush rugs. Liko imagined that each rug probably cost more than his mother's trailer.

He now understood the value of the Niihau necklace his aunt had given his mother. It must have been very valuable. An heirloom. Yet his father had sold it and gambled away the money.

Thinking about his father and remembering his rum-drunk mother, a wave of shame overcame him. How could he allow himself to return to that life?

Liko dropped into a rattan chair on the backyard lanai, and Auntie and Keahi sat down in a rattan couch, together. Keahi placed his hand on his aunt's and listened to himself chanting, while Liko, his big body overflowing the chair, surveyed the magnificent backyard. A yardman was repairing one of the tall stone walls that separated Auntie's yard from her neighbors. A hedge with bright red flowers had been allowed to grow ten feet high. The hedge hid most of the wall. It was a thorny, seemingly impenetrable barrier.

"Liko, you see those bright red flowers?" Auntie asked.

"Yes."

"Well, those aren't bright red flowers. Those are leaves that look like flowers."

"No kidding?" Liko said.

"They are bougainvillea bracts. Bracts, not leaves."

A breeze brushed Keahi's cheeks. He continued to listen to himself chanting. "I should have continued my music."

"No one had a more beautiful voice," his aunt agreed. Then turning back to Liko, "Your uncle won three years in a row at the Hoku-alihi Festival."

And then I squandered my gift, my voice, Keahi thought.

Liko politely asked the direction to the bathroom and excused himself.

After he left, Auntie smiled at Keahi. "Are you enjoying being a parent for the summer?"

The question surprised Keahi. "He's behaving himself."

"You'd make a good father."

Keahi was incredulous. "You're the second person in the last twenty-four hours who's told me that."

Auntie looked carefully at Keahi. A curious expression filled her sun-tanned face.

"Angelica," Keahi answered. "Angelica said that I would make a good father."

"Oh," she said, slightly nodding her head, smiling in a knowing way.

"Liko is straight?" she asked.

"Yes. Why?"

"Gay genes run on the maternal side of the family. More men on the maternal side are gay. I think you inherited gay genes from your mother."

"I see." Keahi was quiet for a moment as he contemplated what she had just said.

"I haven't heard that theory before. But if you are correct, and gay genes are maternal, then she could have passed gay genes through to Liko. Wouldn't that be ironic?"

"Yes, the one person who has never accepted you for who you are."

Keahi reflected on how cruel his sister had been to him when he was still at home, before he had found refuge in his aunt's house. She had a mean nature that presented itself through derogatory, hurtful, yet often truthful comments. If there was a maternal effect it would be ironic, indeed. But he doubted the gene connection.

"He's a handsome boy. He has his father's strong features."

"Well, let's hope he doesn't have his weaknesses, too."

And then they were quiet for a moment, like two old friends who were comfortable with each other's company. He continued to hold his aunt's hand, affectionately.

"Something seems to be troubling you," Auntie ventured, gently squeezing his hand.

"Have you been reading the papers?"

"Yes," she said, with concern in her voice. "You mean the explosion at the playground?"

"Yes. You know a boy died."

She nodded.

And then Liko reentered the room, wearing a mask and carrying a war club. "There is a bowl back there with teeth mounted in it," he announced. "Are they human teeth?"

"That mask is a rare piece." The tone of Auntie's voice suggested that Liko should be very careful with it. "And yes, they *are* human teeth. A victorious warrior sometimes mounted the teeth of his enemies on his warrior bowl."

Keahi stared at Liko in the warrior mask. He didn't like what he saw. A furtive glance at his aunt assured him that she wasn't pleased, either.

"Liko, have you been to the Pali?" Auntie asked.

Liko shook his head, no.

"Well, today is a good day. Today Keahi should take you there. Many warriors died at the Pali."

Liko removed the mask and gently set it and the warrior club on a nearby table.

"What would you like to do after you graduate from high school?" Auntie asked.

"Travel. I'd like to travel around the world."

Both Keahi and Auntie looked at each other and couldn't contain their smiles. They chuckled—the family chuckle.

"Well, young man," Auntie said, "after you have traveled around the world, then you may decide to go to college?"

Liko thought about his mom wanting him to stay with her in the trailer park. Now his aunt was suggesting he attend a university. It seemed as if everyone was plotting against him, trying to control his life.

"Maybe, but I haven't decided yet."

"Your Uncle Keahi is a good man. He has a good heart. But do not do what he has done and squander the natural gifts you have inherited. And do not turn your back on whatever opportunities come your way!"

Keahi winced. Her words cut deep. "I just haven't found what I'm looking for."

Auntie rolled her eyes and chuckled softly, again.

Yes, he had squandered his youth in Honolulu, partying, having a good time, instead of training with his *kumu hula*. He had been naïve and foolish. He knew all that. But to hear it spoken, especially by his aunt, that hurt!

For years Auntie had tried to get him to return to his music and dance, to start performing again. And for years he had ignored her. It was only now, seeing Liko in his youthfulness and with his whole life ahead of him, that Keahi realized his grave mistake. Complacency was a thief. And now he was in his fifties. He felt unexpected tears begin to well up in his eyes. *My God*, he thought, *I* am *becoming a weepy gay widow!*

"If you will excuse me, I need to use the restroom. I'll be back in a minute." Auntie nodded and Keahi rose from the rattan chair and disappeared down the large hallway.

"Sometimes you have to make your own luck, Liko," Auntie said, after Keahi disappeared. "And you must constantly be on the lookout for opportunities. And you *must* seize each opportunity that comes your way!"

Yes, Liko understood.

"Liko, someday you will attend a university, and when you do, don't take classes that will lead to a government job. The truly good jobs, for people like you and Joe and Keahi," she paused, thinking about Keahi, "are not government jobs.

"Look at Singapore, Indonesia, and even India. The college graduates of those countries become bureaucrats. I've heard the same thing is happening in Africa. Even colleges in China breed bureaucrats. And the last thing the world needs is another bureaucrat!

"No matter what the consequences," she said, "pursue your dream. Your own unique dream."

They chatted until Keahi returned and sat down in his rattan chair. "We have a dive coming up," he put in.

"A dive?" Auntie asked. Then, without waiting for an answer, she proceeded to tell Liko all about *Kanaloa*, the Hawaiian lord of the ocean. And then she talked about *Kane*, another Hawaiian god, until it was time for them to leave.

As they left, Auntie handed Keahi a CD: a recording of his chants that had won the Hoku-alihi Festival. It was his winning performance that she had just played for them.

Keahi sighed. *Poor Auntie, she is still keeping my dreams for me.*

CHAPTER SEVEN

AN INNER VOICE WAS SCREAMING for Liko to yank his face out of the water and to rip off his mask and snorkel.

But Uncle Keahi had insisted, and Liko would not disappoint. Why? They had an agreement. Keahi wanted a dive partner for the summer; Liko wanted a ticket out of the trailer park. So here he was, 7am, at Hanauma Bay Nature Reserve, with Keahi, Carol and Angelica, snorkeling. And he couldn't swim.

Liko raised his head out of the water carefully, and surveyed the surface of the bay. It appeared calm—almost flat, with small waves. He stood up and his tiptoes touched rubble and sand. A small wave reached his chin.

He was not enjoying himself. He could float and dogpaddle, but that was it.

Balancing on his toes, he glanced all around through his fogged-up mask. He was in a horseshoe-shaped bay inside the steep-walled crater of an extinct volcano. According to the introductory film, which newcomers to Hanauma Bay were required to watch in the educational center before they were allowed to snorkel, thousands of years ago waves had eroded the volcano's outer seawall causing the seawall to collapse, opening the volcano to the ocean.

Balancing on his toes, Liko also saw that he was twenty feet from shore, between a white sandy beach and a protective coral reef. Beyond the living reef was the breached wall of the volcano and deep, blue water. Seeing the wide breach, and standing in the ocean while inside an extinct volcano, he was astounded. It was incredible. Awe-inspiring.

He searched for Keahi, Angelica and Carol and saw them together further down the crescent-shaped reef, snorkeling. Determined to keep up with them, he snorkeled in their direction, passing over flat-topped coral boulders whose white tops came to within a foot of the surface, and dogpaddled between coral boulders in water over his head.

As he floated over a sun-bleached boulder a sudden movement startled him. It was a brown creature as big as Liko's head, half-hidden in a crevice, a foot-and-a-half from his face.

He felt an adrenaline rush.

He saw large eyes in an alien-like brown body that retreated deeper into the shadows of the crevice, but not before Liko saw tentacles, each with two parallel rows of round suckers.

He raised his head just above the water and yelled, "Hey, take a look at this!" But his voice was muffled by his mask, so Keahi, Angelica and Carol, huddled only twenty feet away, didn't hear him.

Excited, holding onto the smooth coral with one hand and dangling over the side of the large boulder, he wrenched off his mask and called out again, louder, "You guys! You've got to see this!"

This time they turned in his direction and Angelica acknowledged him with a friendly wave of her hand.

Keahi snorkeled over first and Liko pointed to the creature. Keahi pushed his mask onto the crown of his head. "It's a *he'e*, an octopus ... hiding in a *puka*, a hole."

Angelica was the next to snorkel over. "It's a big one, maybe two feet. You usually see smaller ones."

"Can it bite?" Liko asked.

"It has a beak," Angelica said, "but it's shy."

"Maybe *you* will bite *it*," Keahi said, chuckling.

"What?" Liko asked, surprised. "Me bite an octopus?" He looked at Keahi incredulously.

"Why not? You *are* Hawaiian. Our ancestors killed *he'e* by biting them on the head."

Liko grimaced.

"Yeah. And pounded 'em with rocks to break their muscles. And eat 'em raw."

He wondered if Keahi was joking.

After Carol snorkeled over and saw the octopus, they all donned their masks and Keahi led them into deeper water. Angelica followed Keahi, Liko trailed Angelica, and Carol brought up the rear. When Keahi found a place he liked, they stopped and hovered quietly on the surface, now three to four feet above the coral heads and ten feet above the sandy sea floor.

Dogpaddling, Liko felt his stomach tense.

Yellow, green, blue, and multi-colored fish appeared from all directions and surrounded them. The fish were different sizes and shapes. Some swam in schools. Some in pairs. A few swam solo. And as they swam among the four floating humans, they were a swirling rainbow.

"Here they don't fear us," Angelica said.

But Liko was not enjoying the experience. Instead, he was concentrating on staying afloat. His whole body was tense.

Angelica tapped his side and signaled him to follow her and he did, consciously kicking with his fins. Soon they were in the open, and a rocky ocean floor lay below them. The water now looked deep—*maybe fifteen feet deep?*

Angelica stopped and pointed out a three-foot long thick-bodied fish butting its head against a coral boulder, making a crunching noise. When Liko looked more carefully, he discovered that the bi-colored fish—a shade of yellow and off-yellow—was actually scraping its large beak across the coral, feeding, not butting. It was the biggest live fish Liko had ever seen.

"What is it?"

Angelica pushed her mask on top of her head. "A parrotfish. Many start life as males, then mature into females. It physically changes sex, from male to female."

"No way," Liko said. He wanted to push his mask on top of his head too, but he needed his hands to tread water, so he left it covering his nose and eyes. His snorkel tube dangled from his mask as he talked. "A sex change?"

"No," Angelica answered. "More like a sex reversal."

Liko looked into her face through the fog of his mask. She was beautiful: long blond hair, green eyes, and a strong, prominent chin. And while following her, Liko had noticed her long legs, her perfect tush, and her globe-shaped breasts hanging.

Liko wished he had a body like Keahi's—muscular with no fat. And a nice tan. At the moment, though, he was thankful for the rash guard he was wearing, because it hid the inflamed pimples on his shoulders and covered the softness of his stomach.

"Come with me," Angelica beckoned. "I'll show you more."

"What about Keahi? And Carol?"

"Ah! Don't worry about them! They are buddy-buddy, and so are we." She smiled.

"Where are we going?"

"Through the reef, through a narrow passage where they laid a communication cable many years ago. It should be easy to get through. The waves are small today and the current is going out."

Before he could protest, Angelica said, "Follow me," and took off snorkeling towards the reef, away from shore. He caught up with her at the narrow passage, where she was waiting for him.

As he floated into position beside her, he felt the water behind him, pushing him towards the narrow opening; there was also a venturi effect, sucking him forward. Then he felt the surge reverse and the water rushed back over him in choppy little waves, pushing him backwards. There was something about the backwards push that annoyed him. Confused waves washed over his head and filled his snorkel and shoved him against Angelica. He felt his skin slide against her skin. He liked that!

Adrenalin flowing, he cleared his snorkel.

When the surge reversed again, he followed her into the funnel. However, he miscalculated and his body scraped against basalt boulders—first one side of his body, then the other. Determined, he pulled himself along. The coral nicked his fingertips, scratched his knees and legs, and scraped against his rash guard. But the pain was masked by the joy he still felt, having rubbed against Angelica. The current suddenly sucked him forward through the end of the funnel and released him into water way over his head.

He dogpaddled after Angelica, anxious to catch up with her. Now the waves came in sets and washed over his head. He blew water out his snorkel.

He trailed Angelica as she followed the outer edge of the reef. She snorkeled effortlessly. He struggled to keep up.

Then she suddenly stopped.

She set her mask on her forehead, pointed in front of her, and yelled, "There! See it? A green sea turtle!"

Liko pushed his mask on top of his head too, while at the same time furiously dogpaddling. His uncoordinated effort failed and he slipped under the surface.

He inhaled saltwater then violently coughed, clearing his windpipe. The saltwater felt rough and burned, which surprised him: wasn't water soft and smooth?

She grabbed his arm and held him up. "You okay?"

"I'm fine." Her strong grip was reassuring, but also embarrassing.

"Always approach a turtle from behind. Stay in its blind spot. It can swim faster than you can run."

With her help, Liko put his mask back on and they hovered

above the turtle for a long time, admiring it. The turtle wore a mottled suit of armor: a brown, olive, gold and black shell. Its beak had a sharp-looking edge.

The turtle began to swim away, slowly, beating its forelimbs like a bird on the wing. *Incredible!* Liko thought. And then to his astonishment, Angelica followed.

Liko shivered. He raised his head above the surface just enough to get his bearings. He could barely make out the orange lifeguard tower on the other side of the fringe reef.

But he followed Angelica and she followed the turtle, which was swimming parallel to the algal ridge, heading towards the lava flow arch just south of where tourists were trekking down a steep asphalt road from the rim of the volcano to the sea, the same road that the four of them had descended earlier that morning. Over there, ahead, the water looked rough: bigger waves, white spray, jagged rocks.

Nevertheless, Angelica followed the turtle as it headed directly towards the turbulent water. Liko snorkeled up beside her, yet slightly behind—within arm's reach. They crossed an underwater canyon. The water was crystal clear. The sunlight was shining on the ocean floor, reflecting off the white sand fifty feet below them. Waves of white sand rested on the ocean floor, motionless.

Then Angelica paused, grabbed her fin, and stretched her leg straight out in front of her. Holding onto her foot, with her leg fully extended, she cursed, "Damnit."

"Are you okay?"

"Yes. I just need to stretch my leg. Get rid of this cramp." Her teeth were chattering. "I thought we could cross the 'back door'—it's somewhere along here—but I don't see it."

Liko looked towards the shore. Back door? What was she talking about? Waves were churning across the reef, which was between them and the shore, and he instinctively knew that they couldn't cross the reef without being shredded. Waves would push them against the sharp coral, and Angelica's bikini was skimpy.

He watched her shiver. He was surprised that she was cold because the water felt fine to him. But then he realized what had happened; he was overweight, insulated by a thick layer of body fat. She wasn't. She was fit and muscular.

He then realized that they would have to snorkel back the way they had come. He felt adrenaline surge through his body. *Should I signal the lifeguard?*

"I'll be right behind you," he said. He hoped his voice sounded encouraging and not as he felt.

They U-turned and headed back, again snorkeling parallel to the shore.

Another minute passed.

Then Angelica stopped. Again she grabbed her fin and stretched out her leg. She dropped below the surface like a rock, descending straight down, fast, still holding the fin in her hands.

Liko watched her grow small below him. Then she jerked. He watched as she struggled, corkscrewing back to the surface. She gasped for air, cussed, grabbed her fin again, thrashed about. And then she sank.

Liko yelled for help, splashing water. He looked toward shore. The orange lifeguard tower was a long ways off. He waved his arms wildly over his head, yelling for help, propelling himself as high above the ocean as possible.

Then he sank, too.

When he stopped struggling, he leveled out ten feet below the surface. *No one heard me. No one saw me.*

As he slowly floated back to the surface, he looked for Angelica and saw her at least three body lengths below him. She was pounding her calf and her thigh with her fists. Her blonde hair floating above her head. Air bubbles flowed upwards, bursting beside him.

Liko had never done a surface dive without a scuba tank, yet he bent at the waist and forced his upper body under the water. He kicked aimlessly in the air and somersaulted onto his back. He squinted in the bright sun. Water in his nose—blasted it away.

He rolled over onto his stomach and tried again to dive. This time he bent at the waist, reached for his toes and descended headfirst. He concentrated. His legs followed his body. His feet reentered the water. He was upside down, head first, looking downward at the ocean floor. He looked for Angelica. He found her, far below. He kicked and this time his fins pushed against water and he descended, ten feet, twenty feet—his ears hurt—thirty feet to Angelica's side.

Her eyes looked as if she no longer occupied her body. He touched her shoulder. She grabbed him. He tried to pull away. She climbed on top of him and wrapped her legs around him. They rolled on the sandy floor. Fine sand billowed upward and enveloped them.

Angelica's arm wrapped around his neck. She choked him from behind. Her grip tightened.

Suddenly, they were yanked apart and he was being pulled to the surface. It was Keahi. He saw Carol pulling

Angelica upward too, holding her from behind.

They broke the surface. A lifeguard was waiting, sitting on his yellow rescue board.

Carol and the lifeguard pulled Angelica over the long rescue board. Water gushed from her mouth. She coughed, vomited, coughed again. She mumbled something. And then she collapsed, laying stomach first across the rescue board.

"I'll get her to shore," the lifeguard said.

"Good," Keahi replied. "I'll get this one in." He wrapped a powerful arm around Liko's chest, reaching around him from behind, and slowly began to pull and swim him back to shore. At first Liko protested and struggled. But Keahi ordered, "Take it easy!"

Keahi mumbled something about Liko not going into shock.

After they passed through the reef, Keahi let Liko dogpaddle the rest of the way to shore.

When they reached shore, the lifeguards had already transported Angelica to the top of the crater. Carol had sprinted up the steep asphalt road after her, almost catching up to the lifeguard's three-wheel vehicle.

Liko felt like he had swallowed curdled milk. He dropped to his knees and vomited.

"How is she?" Keahi asked a lifeguard who had stayed behind.

"She'll be okay, but they're taking her to the hospital just as a precaution."

"That was scary," Keahi said, standing over Liko. "She's one of the best swimmers I know."

"She got cold," Liko said. "She started cramping." Kneeling on the beach with his head hanging down, Liko thought he might vomit again.

Placing a gentle hand on Liko's shoulder, Keahi said, "Never approach someone who is drowning from the front unless you are much bigger and stronger, like me. Even then it is dangerous." Then the tone of Keahi's voice changed from one of fatherly admonishment to one of teasing. "You are bigger, but she is stronger."

Liko was embarrassed.

Later that evening, Liko and Keahi were sitting side-by-side in the lounge chairs on Keahi's lanai, having canceled their plans to barbecue a'u. Instead, Keahi had thrown the fresh fish into the freezer, mumbling, "It won't keep."

Liko shivered as if he was cold, yet it was a warm evening. Keahi noticed the shivering but didn't comment on it. He took another swig of Foster's Lager and asked, "What happened out there?"

Liko's stomach was still sour. He scrunched his shoulders around his neck, trying to relax stiff neck muscles. He let his shoulders drop.

Feeling unsure, he blamed Angelica. "She overextended herself. She got cold and her leg cramped."

"Why did you go out so far?"

"It was her idea, not mine."

From Keahi's puzzled expression, Liko knew that he

needed to explain in more detail. "We were following a turtle."

"You know that Carol and I looked for you guys? We didn't know where you had gone."

"Hey, it was Angelica's idea. I didn't want to go, but she insisted."

For a brief moment Liko thought about telling Keahi the truth: that he felt uncomfortable in water over his head, that he was a terrible swimmer, and that his obesity had staved off his own hypothermia. Instead, he said, "We tried to make it back. But her cramps got worse. And then she went under."

He looked at Keahi and anxiously waited for his reaction. He didn't want to disappoint him. He needed his approval.

But when Keahi didn't say anything, Liko decided that he needed to explain further: "When she went under ... the second time ... she sank like a rock. She was holding her leg. She dropped straight down. I dove after her and tried to bring her back to the surface, but..." His explanation hung, unfinished.

Keahi thought about that. He stretched out his arm and put his hand on Liko's shoulder and patted him.

"Your father," Keahi said, "he once rescued a military guy off Makua Beach. Broke the guy's jaw and cracked two of his ribs." Keahi looked at Liko. "An offshore rip pulled the guy out and he tried to swim back to shore against the current. Wore himself out in deep water. Flapped his arms and screamed like he was being stung by jellyfish and then he went under. Your father swam out to help him. The guy was confused and panicked. He tried to pull your father under, too. That's when your dad knocked him out. They had to wire the guy's jaw."

Liko sat back wearily, unhappy that his dad had been brought into the conversation. His current problem, his inability to swim, had nothing to do with his dad.

Keahi warned in a stern voice, "If someone is drowning, always approach them from behind. Even if you are bigger and stronger."

"Or knock the shit out of them, the way my dad did?"

Keahi was surprised at the bitterness in Liko's voice.

"Are you up to the dives next weekend?" Because of the accident, they had moved tomorrow's dive out a week.

Was he? He wasn't sure.

Liko looked at Keahi. Keahi had given him the plane ticket to Hawaii, let him stay at his place, and now he had saved his life. *I owe him big time. And I don't want to disappoint him further.*

Keahi repeated his question, "Are you up to the dives?"

"Sure, why not?"

"Good. For a moment I thought I would have to return this." Keahi reached behind his blue and white striped lounge chair and pulled out a large box wrapped in bright yellow paper with a thick, red ribbon. "It's from Auntie."

Speechless, Liko accepted the package and ripped the paper off in one smooth motion, revealing a box with a picture on the cover—a black buoyancy control jacket.

As Liko opened the box and took out the jacket, Keahi said, "It's a nice vest, expensive. Top of the line. Auntie knows how important it is to have dependable gear."

Liko wanted to say, "I'm a dead man." Instead, still shivering, he said, "I'll call her first thing tomorrow morning and thank her."

CHAPTER EIGHT

As Keahi stepped into the breakroom to fill his coffee mug, he thought, *I hope I don't run into Kwon or Masako this morning.* He wanted to hear nothing more about the sinking of the Tsushima Maru, the sneak attack on Pearl Harbor, or the atomic bombing of Hiroshima and Nagasaki. He didn't want to think about children drowning or sailors burning or people vaporizing. All he wanted was a cup of Kona Gold coffee. He had gotten up late and missed his usual two cups at home, and he was feeling tired.

"Good morning, Keahi," a woman's voice said, startling him.

He spun around and was relieved to see Toi, not Masako.

"Toi! Howzit?"

"Good, and how was your weekend?"

Keahi smiled. He loved the sound of Toi's voice. The warbling inflections, the mixed French-Vietnamese accent, the happy tones, such sounds were music to Keahi. *Toi has the voice of a songbird*, he thought.

"I went snorkeling at Hanauma Bay."

"Sounds fun."

"No, it was terrible! My friend Angelica almost drowned!" Keahi shook his head. "She got cold and her leg cramped."

At that moment, Masako entered the break room. She was wearing a loose, red tunic and silky black pants. A moment later, Kwon burst in. He was wearing red suspenders over an aloha shirt with a reddish-tan and yellow pattern of taro. His black hair was messed up and reversed forward. Keahi imagined a small hyena about to pull down a graceful antelope.

As Toi filled her electric tea kettle at the sink, Keahi said, "Let me help you."

"Thanks, but I can manage."

"No, I insist." Keahi reached for the kettle, lifted it out of her hands, and hurried her towards the door. "I'll walk you back to your cubicle."

His sudden movements startled her yet she acquiesced. "Okay," she said.

He acknowledged Masako and Kwon with a tip of his head, but he deliberately said nothing to them. Instead, he hurried past them carrying the tea kettle and exited with Toi through the door and headed down the hall.

A narrow escape, he thought.

"Next weekend Liko and I have a night dive."

"I thought you quit diving."

Keahi held the door for her as they entered the Water Unit. "I did, but he just got his scuba license, so I signed us up for some dives. I thought he'd like to try a deep dive and maybe even a night dive."

When they reached Toi's cubicle, he handed her the electric teakettle. She plugged it in and set it on top of the low, two-drawer file cabinet beside her desk. Then she placed a bag of green tea in a white porcelain cup that had a picture of a porpoise on it.

Keahi ran his eyes over her University of Hawaii diploma: a Master's degree in Marine Biology. It was inexpensively framed and hung to the right of her desk next to a picture of two butterfly fish. Toi had covered the walls of her cubicle with framed photographs of undersea life.

He sat down in the guest chair. "Nice pictures."

"It's my hobby."

"They look professional."

"Thanks. Occasionally I sell a photo. It helps pay for the dives."

Then Toi asked, "How are things without Pete?"

"Not so good. I miss him."

"Have you heard from him?"

"No."

"And the explosion?" Toi asked. "Anything new?"

"I discovered that an old service station operated on the site."

"Really?"

"Yeah, I checked the Fire Marshal's archives and found an aerial photograph taken in the fifties. A gas station's footprint covers the playground. So there may be an old fuel tank. A gasoline tank. Kwon and I are working on it."

"And if you find one?"

"We'll order the current property owner to remove it and to clean up any gasoline release. But we also need to check the neighbor's properties." Keahi paused and frowned. "Unfortunately, to extend the investigation off-site, I need Santos's approval." He sighed.

"I call him the arandapsis."

"What?"

"My nickname for Santos," Toi explained. "I call him the arandapsis."

"Aranwhatsis?"

"Arandapsis. It's an extinct fish."

Keahi looked at her with a puzzled expression, which caused her to blush.

"An arandapsis had a round, sucker-like mouth, no teeth, no jaws."

"Ar-an-dap-sis. Ar-an-dap-sis." Keahi smiled. "That sounds like the wheezing noise he makes when he gets excited, yeah? I like that—arandapsis." He chuckled and Toi laughed.

"I heard about Little Bill, too," Toi said.

Keahi nodded his head. His eyes roamed over Toi's underwater photographs and came to rest on a picture of whitetip sharks.

"Sorry," Toi added.

Keahi acknowledged her condolence with a nod of his head.

"Liko can't swim?"

"Not very good. He's a poor swimmer."

"No!" Toi looked at Keahi thoughtfully. "And he's going on a deep dive?"

Keahi nodded his head, yes. "I noticed it at Hanauma Bay. He's a dogpaddler."

"Then he has no business scuba diving." Toi was giving him a serious, concerned look.

And then her phone rang.

"I'll see you later," he said, abruptly excusing himself, leaving her to answer the phone.

As he left the Water Unit, he glanced up and down the hallway. Masako and Kwon were not in sight. He hoped they had already returned to their units—Kwon to Air and Masako to Hazardous Waste.

He especially didn't want to run into Kwon. Kwon's nasty attitude towards Masako puzzled him. It was straining their relationship.

On his way back to his cubicle, Keahi saw the arandapsis at the Xerox machine, watching paper spew out of the copier. He appeared transfixed by the automatic collating feature. His shoulders drooped forward and his short, fat arms hung at his side, as if useless.

"Howzit?" Keahi asked as he approached.

"What is it?" The tone of Santos's voice sounded whiny, as if he was soliciting pity and had actually said, "My job is so difficult I deserve special recognition." He shifted his body so that he was facing the copier, squarely, with his back to Keahi. *He has no neck*, Keahi thought, noticing that Santos's oversized head seemed to rest directly on his rounded shoulders, like a hippo.

"I need to do additional site characterization at the child care center."

"Why?"

"I think the soil beneath the playground is saturated with gasoline, just below the surface. The organic vapor analyzer showed high readings."

"Gasoline?" There was a derogatory tone in Santos's voice. "At a child care facility?"

"It used to be a gas station."

Santos glanced over his rounded shoulder and briefly made eye contact with Keahi. His lips became pouty.

"Been playing detective, huh?"

Ignoring Santos's jibe, Keahi explained, "We need to bring in a Geoprobe and collect soil and groundwater samples in the playground."

Santos said nothing. He opened a small latched cover on top of the copier and pushed a button and the copier began stapling.

"We also need to extend the investigation off-site, uphill to a former laundry, where the Kesago Club is now."

Santos turned and faced Keahi. "You want my permission to run around the neighborhood drilling holes everywhere?"

"No. No—of course not. We would start with the hand-held organic vapor analyzer and just probe accessible *pukas* for explosive vapors—like sewer manholes and underground utility vaults."

"And if you find vapors, then what?"

"Then we bring in the Geoprobe."

"We?" Santos made a puffing sound as if he was suddenly short of breath. Santos was in such poor physical condition that Keahi wondered if he would live to see his retirement. "Who is 'we?'" Santos puffed again, then took a deep breath and said, "You keep saying, 'we.'"

Arandapsis, Keahi thought. *Arandapsis.*

"Kwon is helping me. He suggested we take organic vapor readings at the Kesago Club. It may be upgradient and—"

"No! Absolutely not!" Santos made a wheezing sound. "You're to stay inside the playground!" Santos paused to catch his breath and then continued. "You don't have to stir up trouble." With that, he turned his back to Keahi again and started collecting the stapled, collated copies from the tray.

"And who gave you permission to involve another unit?"

"Kwon helped me with the survey—I used the OVA and he followed and recorded the vapor readings. The OVA—it's bulky and heavy. It's hard to carry it and also juggle a clipboard and pen and record vapor readings."

"If he is doing your work, then who is doing his?"

Keahi noted that the stack of copies was growing tall on top of the copier. He hated paperwork. *Maybe I should quit, just like Pete. Why not?*

"I think we need to investigate the Kesago Club because it used to be a laundry," he said, trying to change the subject back to the investigation and away from Kwon. "In the old days, laundry operations had their own fuel tanks. A plume of gasoline could have—"

Santos interrupted. He often interrupted. "For your information, I already know about the laundry site. I closed the tanks there. There is no problem there. It was investigated and cleaned up years ago. They had a heating oil tank that they used to heat water for washing laundry. And it was a diesel release, not gasoline. And in case you have forgotten, we do not regulate heating oil tanks. They are exempt from federal *and* state underground storage tank regulations. So case closed!"

Keahi thought, *I shouldn't have to go through this.* He said, "I've already called the owner of the night club and set up a meeting with his consultant, someone named Alegado. I'm meeting them later this morning."

"What? No you're not!" Santos was wheezing again. He groaned and slid the copies into his arms, onto his big stomach. Then he turned around to face Keahi.

Keahi shifted his feet. His steel toe work boots suddenly felt oversized. "It's too late to cancel the meeting. It's scheduled for this morning. It's—"

Santos's face filled with disapproval.

"I know," Keahi said, biting his tongue. "I know I should have cleared it with you first."

Santos's expression was changing to anger.

"Okay. I'll call and try to cancel—but they may have left already."

"Left for where?"

"We were going to meet at a hotel coffee shop."

"I'm surrounded by idiots!" Santos was furious.

"Hey, I said I'll try to cancel. I thought it was important to determine the cause of the explosion as quickly as we could, and that meant pursuing all possible causes."

Santos stormed off carrying the copies, his short arms straight in front of him, elbows locked, and his shoulders bowed forward.

No wonder he has bad posture, Keahi thought.

Alone, standing beside the copier, Keahi said out loud, "Damnit! If I'm going to make a mistake, I'm going to err on the side of the kids."

Keahi was surprised when Santos entered his cubicle ten minutes later and told him *not* to cancel the meeting. Instead, Santos said he would accompany him to the coffee shop to meet the owner of the Kesago Club. Keahi was even more surprised when Santos said, "Afterwards, we will drive out to the child care center."

What would it be like to spend a day in the field with Santos?

They rode in his white Park Avenue Ultra to the hotel, where he valet parked. Then they rode a glass-walled elevator overlooking the lobby up to the third floor. They passed several souvenir and fashion boutiques, and then, finally, entered the coffee shop.

A waitress led them to a spacious lanai, sunlit and open to ocean breezes. The dining area had a Banana Republic feeling: large rattan chairs with colorful cushions, round tables covered with white cotton tablecloths, ironed. Small palm trees in large planters created a feeling of privacy.

The only diners on the lanai were two men and a young boy, who was grade school age. Keahi guessed that the man wearing the gold necklace was the club owner, and that the man with the legal pad and Mont Blanc pen was his consultant, Alegado. The consultant was wearing a gray silk shirt.

"You must be Alegado?"

"Yes." Alegado looked Keahi in the eye and took his hand like a politician, pumping it up and down three times and slightly squeezing his fingers. Eyes like an eel, his expression disdainful, his black hair slicked back.

Keahi immediately disliked him.

"I'm Keahi. And this is Santos Baniaga, my supervisor at the department."

"I go by Santos," Santos said to Alegado with a forced smile.

"And this is the Captain, the owner of the Kesago Club," Alegado said, introducing his employer.

Keahi extended his hand to the Captain, who shook it limply. He had sharp black eyes and loose black hair and a whey-colored face with chiseled oriental features.

"And this is one of my many grandsons," the Captain said, extending a long finger towards the boy.

The small boy frowned at the sudden attention. There were dark shadows under his eyes. He jabbed at the *loco moco junior* on his plate with a fork, and the small hamburger slid in the gravy on top of the rice.

Santos walked around the rattan table and sat down to the right of the Captain. Keahi took the only chair remaining, between the boy and the consultant, Alegado.

When Keahi sat down, the boy gave him the stink eye.

"Captain, would you by chance live at Black Point Beach?" Keahi asked.

"Yes. How did you know?"

"Just a lucky guess. My great-aunt lives at Black Point Beach too. She mentioned a neighbor she called 'The Captain.' And she said he owned a nightclub."

The Captain's black eyes focused intently on Keahi.

"My great-aunt—"

Alegado interrupted, cutting Keahi off mid-sentence. "When you called, you said you had some questions regarding the Captain's club, the Kesago Club?"

"Not exactly," Keahi replied, taken aback by Alegado's abruptness. "I'm not interested in the club—I'm interested in the laundry that used to be there."

"The Captain is in the entertainment business," Alegado said. "We don't launder."

Alegado smiled, and the Captain threw him a quick look, then broke out in a humorless laugh. "That is funny, very funny," he said. Santos laughed too, but Keahi did not—it was a lame joke.

Keahi noted that as the Captain laughed, he was also staring at him. It was a direct and piercing stare that made him uncomfortable.

He is very focused, Keahi thought.

"As you may be aware, there was an explosion on your neighbor's property in the playground at Kehena Kare," Keahi explained. "The department is investigating the cause of that explosion."

When the Captain and his consultant didn't say anything, Keahi continued. "Based on a preliminary survey using an organic vapor analyzer, we concluded that gasoline vapors may have caused the explosion. However, the source of the vapors is unknown."

Keahi looked at Santos and then at the Captain. *He is studying my voice, the movement of my hands, my facial expressions.*

Keahi went on. "It is possible that the vapors came from off-site. And our records indicate a heating oil underground fuel tank—"

Santos interjected, "I'm sorry. I just learned about this meeting this morning. If I had known earlier, I could have saved all of us this trouble."

Keahi was shocked at Santos's sudden interruption.

"Captain, sir, I explained to Keahi this morning that heating oil tanks are not federally regulated. I also explained to him that your property—the former laundry site—was already investigated." Santos turned to Keahi and said, "In fact, Alegado here was the consultant on the investigation." He turned back to the Captain. "And I explained that a small diesel release from a heating oil tank was reported to us and was cleaned up years ago. At that time, I remember having telephone discussions with Alegado concerning the small tank he removed and his investigation and the cleanup. Although we don't regulate heating oil tanks, I remember giving Alegado advice and answering his questions about how to dispose of a small amount of diesel-contaminated soil. If I remember correctly, the soil was taken to a landfill."

"Yes," Alegado answered, "That is correct."

"Unfortunately, I wasn't aware that Keahi was interested or I would have explained all this to him earlier. Like I said, I'm sorry. I didn't know that he had arranged this meeting until this morning. Anyway, I am satisfied that gasoline could not have come from your property. Especially since the property was cleaned up. Am I correct?" He looked at the Captain's consultant.

"Absolutely," Alegado replied. "I did the work myself. There is no contamination whatsoever on the property at the Kesago Club."

"Is there a closure report documenting the removal of the tank and the contaminated soil?" Keahi asked.

"No," Alegado answered. "It was not a regulated tank. At the time we did the work, closure reports were not required. However, I assure you that all the work was done. Moreover, it was done according to today's standards, as explained to me on the phone by Santos, here." He paused and smiled. "Keahi, you'll just have to trust me."

"It's a clean site," Santos reiterated.

Keahi felt humiliated. "Well, do you know anything that might be useful for our investigation? Anything about the area? For instance, when you were removing the tank, did you notice anything unusual about the geology? Anything that might help us track down the cause of the explosion?"

"No," Alegado replied, leaning into the side of his chair. "I can't think of anything." He stared with his mouth partly open, as if ready to bite if the conversation continued.

Frustrated, Keahi started tapping his spoon against the tablecloth. Then he turned to the boy and said, "You are a lucky boy to have a grandfather who takes you to breakfast at such a nice coffee shop."

The boy said, "I don't think so," and then drowned his *loco moco* in coconut syrup.

"What's your name?" Keahi asked.

The boy replied by knocking over his large glass of milk, which flowed over the edge of the table and made a white waterfall into Keahi's lap.

"I'm sorry," the boy said, first smiling, then flinching.

Keahi jumped up, his pants wet. Soaked, he excused himself to the men's room.

As soon as he left, the Captain turned to Alegado, "What do you think?"

"He's a hopeless bureaucrat," Alegado said, straightening his body, moving forward, then leaning into the opposite side of his chair. "Best not to try and bribe this one."

"Bureaucrat? Yes," the Captain said. "Hopeless? No. I sense something different about this one."

The Captain turned his sharp eyes on Santos.

"Captain, my sincere apology that things got this far."

Alegado moved forward in his chair and summoned a waiter to change the soaked tablecloth.

When Santos first met the Captain, many years ago, Santos had been working in the sewer department. As part of his job back then, Santos reviewed proposed subdivision plats, checking the specifications of proposed roads and sewers to ensure that they met city and county standards. Often he had driven through proposed subdivisions and looked around.

And he had checked the neighboring properties, too. This had not been part of his job, but Santos found it very profitable. The value of the land around a new subdivision—or a new road, for that matter—increased, often substantially. And the draft plans that Santos reviewed were so preliminary that the public did not even know about them. Santos had shared this inside information with the Captain. And in those days, Santos had a real estate license.

Although Santos never had much money, he had information. The Captain and others who *had* money profited from that information by forming *huis* and purchasing nearby land and businesses or homes just before the land prices skyrocketed. Today, things were more complicated; nevertheless, it was almost as easy to turn a profit. The public never knew half of what was going on in the planning department. But the insiders knew.

"What are we going to do about my Club?"

Alegado moved more forward in his chair and answered. "As you requested, I looked into it. The diesel tank was removed several years ago. But there *is* an old gasoline tank— one the laundry used to fuel its delivery trucks. It's still there. It wasn't removed because it was under the parking lot."

Santos was startled. "I didn't know there was a second tank."

"We'll remove it before some hopeless bureaucrat discovers it," Alegado said, jokingly.

"And...?" the Captain asked.

"Hell," replied Alegado, "without a gasoline tank he can't connect the explosion to your club. There is no record of the tank. He will be forced to conclude that the gasoline came from the former service station."

"But the child care center is downhill," Santos protested. "If there is gasoline, Keahi could trace the plume back up the hill."

"That's your problem, Santos." Alegado looked carefully at Santos to make sure he understood. He handed him a business card.

Santos nodded as he took the card. He already knew that it wasn't Alegado's business card. It was a business card for Kalele Lab, a laboratory that Alegado used often.

"I'm depending on you," the Captain warned. "Can I depend on you?"

"Yes, you can depend on me."

"Good."

Keahi returned from the restroom, the front of his pants still wet. He retook his seat.

Keahi asked Alegado if he knew the history of the businesses in the area, or anything at all that would suggest someone might have used a flammable substance.

Alegado undulated backward in his chair and said he couldn't recall anything. His mouth was slightly open and his teeth bared, which Keahi found disconcerting.

Keahi passed out his business cards, and he asked Alegado and the Captain to call if they thought of anything.

The boy gave Keahi a smug look that said, "You're a zero," and rolled his eyes towards the ceiling.

Keahi decided he disliked the boy. In fact, he disliked everyone at the table.

It was a short drive in Santos's big Buick from the hotel to the child care center, but Keahi thought it would take forever. He fidgeted in the leather-trimmed seat and drummed his fingers on the wide leather armrest between Santos and him.

He glanced sideways at Santos. His massive body seemed to have melted into the driver's seat.

"Nice seats," Keahi said.

"They're ten-way adjustable."

"I like my air conditioning cold," Santos went on. "In front of you is a dual temperature control. You can turn down the AC on your side, and I can turn it up on mine."

While Keahi adjusted the climate on his side of the big Buick, Santos put on a Ka'au Crater Boys compact disc, punched up the sound through a nine speaker system, and sang along to the words of the first song, "All I have to offer you is me."

As the air began to circulate, Keahi wondered, *What is that odor?*

He was pissed that Santos had embarrassed him in front of the Captain and Alegado. He felt like confronting Santos, but instead he sat quietly and reviewed their conversation.

Only one other expression got Keahi's attention faster than "trust me," and that was "it's failsafe." Just look what had happened to the oil rig in the Gulf. "Trust me" was a phrase you should never say to a regulator. And Alegado had said "trust me."

Could the odor be Santos's shoes? The stench was unbearable. "Do you mind if I roll down the window?"

"And lose the air conditioning?" The tone of Santos's voice said: "Are you crazy?"

He was driving slowly, as if he was on a leisurely Sunday drive. Keahi calculated that it would take them another twenty minutes to meander to the child care center. Good God! He bit his tongue, and in spite of the sour smell he managed to maintain his self-control, barely.

Finally they reached Kahena, a neighborhood known by locals as the Ellis Island of Hawaii. During the last century, immigrants had moved to this neighborhood to avoid starvation, to escape political unrest and revolutions and wars, and to find a better job and a better life. It was all part of the Great American Dream. And for many immigrants, Kahena was the beginning, middle and end of that dream.

Keahi and Santos drove down a trash-strewn street. A newspaper blew across the fissured asphalt. As they drove around a corner, a dark brown dog barked at the big Buick. Keahi watched as the dog followed a small boy down the sidewalk. A short rope dragged from the dog's neck. The boy, who was holding a stick, watched the big Buick drive by. Then the boy turned around and struck the dog, which rolled over on its back, cowering.

Déjà vu. It reminded Keahi of a short story he had read, but he couldn't remember the name of the story or the author. It was something about a little brown dog.

Kids stopped their games in the street and watched the big, shiny Buick pass silently through their working class neighborhood. Santos drove slowly, avoiding potholes that had been patched and repatched in an endless cycle. The asphalt was like a washboard.

As Santos drove up to the child care center in his sleek Park Avenue Ultra, wearing an expensive, gaudy, gold-banded watch, Keahi felt nauseated.

Santos took two parking spaces near the front door.

Keahi followed Santos into the child care facility. Santos's shoulders were slouched forward, his short arms straight at his side, and he had no movement in his hips.

How can a guy walk that way?

They opened the front door and stepped into a short hallway. No one was present to greet them.

Small cubbies lined both sides of the hallway from the floor to Keahi's waist. The cubbies were three high and each had the name of a child displayed in black magic marker on a rectangular cardboard name placard. The cubbies were crammed full of children's stuff: little shoes, sweaters, toys.

Santos and Keahi sauntered down the hall, passing doorways to empty offices. Then they entered a very large room, which was partitioned into babysitting areas by waist-high wooden barriers. Placards identified the age group of the children in each area: two-year-olds, three-year olds, infants and toddlers.

Unshielded overhead lights were dimmed and the large room was quiet.

In the far corner, in the infant area, they saw the head and shoulders of a man sitting in a rocking chair, facing them behind a cubbie wall, rocking back and forth.

"Hello," Santos called out as they crossed the room to the man.

The man looked up, seemed surprised, then replied, "Come on in." Then as if in hindsight, he added, "What can I do for you?"

"We're looking for the administrator or someone else in charge," Santos said.

"That would be me." The man stood up, pressing a sleeping

infant against his barrel chest. The high back hard maple rocker, suddenly empty, rocked violently back and forth on the black and white tiles. "My wife is the administrator, but she's out sick today, so I'm substituting."

"I'm Santos Baniaga and this is Keahi. We're from the Department of Water, Wind and Sun."

Keahi and Santos gave the man their business cards.

The man studied the cards for a moment, which gave Keahi a chance to study the man closely: he had a youthful face, untouched by the sun, a smile that rested on thin lips, and skin the color of buttermilk. He put the cards in his pocket.

"Nice to meet you both. My name is Pablo."

"Where is everybody?" Santos asked.

"The three-year-olds are on a field trip to the park." He read the business card. "You're from the department? So you already know about our playground and the explosion? Someone from your department was out here earlier this week and told my wife that the playground was off limits to the kids. Said it was unsafe, so we've been taking the three- and four-year-olds to the park. And that leaves me to care for the infants."

Keahi doubted that the public park was any safer for the *keiki*, the kids, than the playground.

"We have a few questions," Santos said.

"Okay, but first I need to change this little girl's diaper. Do you mind if I work while we talk? It's hard to keep up with all these infants!"

Keahi counted five cribs and four sleeping infants. He was thankful they were asleep.

"Who is the owner?" Santos asked.

"We are," Pablo replied. "Besides running the center, my wife and I are also buying the property."

"Oh," Santos said, smiling graciously. "My wife and I own a residential adult care home in Pulekakoli."

"So you understand what it's like to run a small business," Pablo said, hopefully. "My wife runs the center Monday through Friday. I help when I'm needed, like today. Friday nights and Saturday afternoons I teach dance classes. Sundays we're closed. Mondays we become a child care center again. It keeps us busy."

"You teach dance in here?" Keahi asked, surveying the room. Toys were strewn on the floor and children's stuff was everywhere.

"The partitions are movable," Pablo replied. "We just push the kid stuff out of the way."

Pablo stepped over to the infant changing table. It was waist high, and a thin, plastic pad covered the table. The pad was white, with brown and yellow stains.

Pablo picked up a pacifier from the plastic pad and set it on a shelf with baby powders, lotions and ointments.

"My wife showed me the newspaper story about your co-worker." Pablo placed the infant girl on her back on the stained pad. "The one who died in the drug lab explosion. That was a terrible thing. Just terrible."

"I'm sorry," he added, after a moment of silence, "but I can't remember his name."

"Little Bill," Keahi said.

"Don't worry about the picture he borrowed."

"Picture?" Keahi asked. "What picture?"

"The picture of our playground, taken the week after it was built, when the swing set was new."

"The picture?" Santos echoed.

"We kept it framed by the front door."

Santos perked up.

Pablo stripped off the infant's clothes, except for the diaper, and set them on the end of the diaper table. She wiggled her legs and waved her arms. Pablo looked around for something, then seemed frustrated. He said to Keahi, "Can you place your hand on her stomach? And keep her from wiggling over the edge? Her mommy left no diapers. Bad mommy. I just need to get a clean diaper. It will take just a minute."

"Sure." Keahi pinned the infant firmly against the center of the table with his big hand.

Santos smirked at him.

Keahi noted an inch-high wooden edging around the perimeter of the table. He doubted that it would prevent the little wiggler from rolling off.

From where he stood, Keahi could see over a waist-high partition into the next children's area, where a placard on the wall said "Two Year Olds." There were three small tables and many small chairs, much too small for an adult to sit in. Books and toys were scattered on an old rug that was frayed and faded. A row of plastic potty chairs sat empty.

So all the kids and child care providers are at the beach park and this guy is alone with five infants?

After a long minute, Pablo returned with a diaper and relieved Keahi, who was, indeed, relieved.

"I don't want anything around that would remind us of that explosion," said Pablo.

Keahi thought, *It's a picture of a swing set in a playground. Big deal. So Little Bill took a morbid souvenir. So what? Picric Pete collected fuel samples; maybe Little Bill collected photos?*

"When we get the insurance money, we'll replace the swing set."

Pablo removed the soiled diaper, wrapped it in a newspaper and dropped it into an unlined diaper disposal container.

He rolled the infant onto her stomach, cleaned her up with a commercial wet wipe, and patted her bottom with a dry paper towel. He repeated the patting—cooing at the infant—and made baby talk.

Then he turned the infant over on her back. Her little feet kicked playfully in the air, while her little hands opened and closed as if she were trying to grasp something. At the same time, her eyes and smile begged for attention.

Keahi thought that she looked comical on her back, naked, kicking her feet in the air.

Pablo seemed to find it greatly amusing, and he gave the infant little taps on her chest to keep her smiling.

She responded to the attention by wriggling her hands and feet and appearing adorable and helpless. She smiled at Pablo and giggled and wiggled her little feet in the air.

"I don't have a change of clothes." He felt inside the infant's wet pants. "A little damp but not too bad. She'll just have to go back into her little britches."

"Do you mind if we look around?" Santos asked. "Take a look at the playground area?"

"No, not at all," Pablo said. "Somebody from your

department was here earlier, talked to my wife, said he was doing a survey."

"It was Kwon and me," Keahi said.

"Who?" Pablo asked.

"My partner and I, we talked to your wife. We checked the playground and found traces of gasoline."

"Gasoline? We had the grass cut a few weeks ago, and I remember that the groundskeeper had a can of gasoline. It was in the bed of his truck."

Keahi raised an eyebrow.

"Other than that, I have no idea. My wife and I certainly don't use gasoline."

Pablo glanced nervously from Keahi to Santos, then back to Keahi, again. "And we haven't used the playground since the explosion."

"There used to be a gasoline station here, in the fifties," Keahi said. "Do you know anything about the service station?"

"No," Pablo shook his head.

Keahi said, "Any signs of an underground tank? Pipes sticking up? Odors?"

"No. Why?"

"Perhaps there is an abandoned tank."

"Really? In the playground? All these years?"

"It's possible," Keahi said. "A plume of gasoline, the right conditions for gasoline vapors to build up. Then a spark or a match . . . ."

"And in our playground?" Pablo moaned, shaking his head.

Keahi and Santos excused themselves, stepped outside, and started walking inside the fenced playground.

Earlier, during the survey, Keahi had explored every foot of the grass. But today he looked closer at the burnt swing set, the slide, the teeter-totter. The equipment was too close together, and it was designed for older children. The slide lacked a deck and handrails at the top. The fulcrum of the seesaw was open and could crush little hands or pinch off fingers. The old wooden climbing equipment was too high above ground. There were jagged splinters on the wooden parts and rust on the metal firefighter's pole.

But that had nothing to do with the place exploding into flames.

The swings were in an area of grass still blackened from the fire. Not even the nutsedge had started to grow back. The paint on the metal swing set had peeled and blistered, and the plastic seats had melted and cracked.

Keahi looked towards the street. A large oleander bush, eight feet tall, grew wild next to the fence between the playground and the street. The oleander had large, attractive pink blossoms and poisonous leaves.

And then Keahi looked in the opposite direction, upgradient, towards the parking lot of the Kesago Club. The parking lot was hidden behind overgrown mock orange bushes, the same kind of tall bushes that surrounded the Honolulu Zoo. He smelled the fragrant scent from its small white blossoms.

As they walked around the playground, Santos became short-winded and started making his usual puffing noises. In between snatched breaths he explained again why it was impossible for contamination to be coming from the Kesago Club. He insisted that there had never been anything up there—he gestured uphill towards the club—except an old heating oil tank and furthermore, that the tank had long since been removed and a small quantity of contaminated soil had been dug up and hauled away, too.

"Let's walk up there and have a look anyway," Keahi suggested.

"No!" Santos exclaimed. "You haven't listened to anything I've said! I'm not going to start bothering all the small businesses in this neighborhood just to satisfy your curiosity." They continued to walk the perimeter of the playground. Keahi slowed his pace to match Santos's.

"Have you heard anything from Pete?" Santos asked.

"No."

"He's an idiot," Santos quipped.

And then he handed Keahi the business card for the Kalele Lab. "Next time you collect soil samples, use this lab."

Early Sunday morning, immediately after the nightclub closed, two large trucks pulled into the Kesago Club parking lot. The flatbed trailer was carrying a backhoe. The dump truck was empty.

Within minutes the drivers unloaded the backhoe and dug through the cracked asphalt to the top of an underground storage tank, two feet below ground level. Soon, the two men—one working the backhoe and the other holding a dim spotlight—uncovered the sides of a steel tank.

After slipping two chains around it, they yanked the rusty tank from the ground; the metal links screeched as they scraped and bit into the metal of the tank. They set the bulky carcass inside the dump truck and hurriedly released the chains.

After that, the man with the spotlight walked back to the excavation and held the light high overhead. Gasoline shone, floating on groundwater, in the bottom of the pit.

The man sent a text message on his cell phone. Moments later a third truck arrived with a load of clean earth that was dumped into the pit, on top of the gasoline sheen. Then the backhoe operator refilled the hole with the excavated earth. When the hole was level, the man holding the spotlight mumbled orders and they reloaded the backhoe onto its trailer. After that, they jumped into their trucks and drove off the property.

The short convoy of trucks rumbled through the otherwise quiet neighborhood. As the dump truck turned a corner, the tank squealed against the side of the bed, and a small amount of gasoline in the bottom of the tank swooshed from one side of the tank to the other. The tank was a rolling bomb, filled with gasoline vapors: explosive and highly flammable.

When the cleaning crew arrived for work at 6:30am, the parking lot was already resurfaced. As the first feral roosters crowed, a custodian threw day-old bread crusts onto the new, shiny black asphalt, and thousands of pigeons, small doves, sparrows and mynahs filled the parking lot.

When the Captain arrived at 10am in his big-body Benz, he found a mess. He fired the custodian. Alegado ordered a small man to wash down the parking lot. And then the yellow shower tree that the birds roosted in was chainsawed.

CHAPTER NINE

LIKO WAS NERVOUS ABOUT PLUNGING into what he considered a dark hell like the quarry he had dived in Nevada, yet here he was, off the Waianae Coast, descending from a small boat to the ocean floor on a night dive.

He followed the anchor line, clearing his ears as he descended feet first, shining his divelight's narrow beam below his feet to ensure that nothing surprised him. A snug lanyard around his wrist secured the heavy dive light.

He reached the ocean floor, forty feet deep. Keahi was immediately behind him.

Chemical light sticks were fastened to dive tanks and snorkels. They bobbed around Liko like fireflies. He thought it surreal, eerie.

I'm sticking with Keahi, he nervously promised himself. And when Keahi swam away from the anchor line, he followed.

A short while later, a diver fired into a *puka*—a hole in the coral—and speared a spectacled parrotfish.

Everyone gathered around the diver and gazed at the dead fish now illuminated by divelights slicing the dark water. The fish was limp, its large, colorful, powerful body pierced through.

Had it been asleep?

Why had it allowed itself to be so vulnerable?

Liko watched the diver and his buddy swim to the surface with their prize, their divelights and glowlights slowly ascending.

Curious if there were other parrotfish sleeping nearby, Liko searched the coral. He found a few small fish, and then a few larger ones, and soon he was completely engrossed with the search—and, consequently, he failed to notice that everyone had swum on, leaving him behind. Even Keahi was gone.

He switched his dive light to high beam and shone it into the darkness. He saw no one.

I've let him down again! He sank onto a ledge of sharp coral; first his shoulder plowed into it, then his ribs. His thin rash guard was little protection. He kicked angrily to right himself and razor-sharp coral lacerated his knee. He shone the flashlight at his knee and saw a flap of loose skin and blood mixing with seawater. *Damn!*

Frustrated, he added air into his jacket until his overweight body lifted off the coral.

How bad am I bleeding?

He shone the flashlight all around him. The end of the beam was pitch black. The coral bed had disappeared.

Am I moving? Ascending? Rocketing to the surface?

He forcefully blew air out of his lungs, blowing even after

his lungs were empty, as if he were exhaling for a lung capacity test and his life depended on the results.

He broke the surface. He ripped out his mouthpiece and inhaled air. Salty, humid air!

He pivoted until he spotted the dive boat.

It had moved.

Damn! He shook his head. *How could I be so stupid! I've got to find Keahi.*

He descended without the anchor line, letting most of the air out of his jacket. The heavy dive tank and weight belt pulled him down. He literally sank, feet first.

He dropped like an anchor. He felt the pressure slowly increase in his ears, like a blood pressure cuff, slowly squeezing, and squeezing, and squeezing. *How much more? Oh my God!*

His ears hurt, so he inflated his jacket. Again he forced the air from his lungs. He resurfaced.

The boat was even further away, which disturbed him.

I've got to find Keahi.

Again he descended, but this time he pinched his nose and worked his jaw and blew air and equalized his ears. Consequently, when he reached the ocean floor his ears were okay.

He's probably looking for me. And he's going to be angry.

No dive lights. No chemical sticks. He searched but found no one. *How long have I searched? I should resurface.*

But this time, when he caught sight of the dive boat, it was much further away.

This is really bad.

He swam for the boat, dogpaddling until he had to stop to

rest. *Should I swim underwater instead? But I can't navigate underwater, especially at night.* He dogpaddled until his heart was pounding in his chest.

He rechecked the position of the boat. It was further away!

The scuba gear is holding me back, he decided, so he dropped his weight belt and added air to his jacket and kicked harder. He was soon exhausted.

Yet the boat light was dimmer. The boat smaller.

Am I being blown downwind? Like an over-inflated ballon blown across the surface of the ocean?

He immediately let some air out of his jacket. Just enough to sink, slightly, yet still keep his head above water.

He watched in horror as the boat's silhouette grew smaller and smaller on the horizon, until it was the size of his thumb.

A current is taking me away from the boat!

He yelled at the top of his lungs, hoping someone on the boat would hear him. He yelled, and yelled, and yelled.

Then the boat disappeared and it occurred to him that he could die.

He considered his chances of dogpaddling against the wind and the current to the dive boat. *What if I remove my jacket? It's the inflated jacket that tricked me.*

Floating on the surface, with the stars above him and no moon, he sighed. *This just isn't right.* He looked at the stars and closed his eyes and shivered.

He reopened his eyes. The physical presence of the ocean and the sky were amazing. The stars were bright and beautiful. He struggled to describe what he was seeing: Magnificent? Endless? Overwhelming?

His right knee ached. He reached down and felt a piece of

loose skin partly covering a lacerated kneecap. *I hurt myself worse than I thought.* He looked at his hand. It was dark but he could discern the gray nuance of blood. He licked his fingertips. It tasted salty, of course. But it also tasted bloody. *I must be bleeding really bad.*

He wondered if the blood would attract sharks, possibly from great distances, especially if he floundered in the water, so he stopped moving.

The idea that he could so easily die annoyed him. He found it embarrassing. It seemed like *everything* and every event was designed to embarrass him.

Minutes passed. Nothing occupied his mind, except his determination to stay alert for sharks, to be ready to fight. He expected them to appear.

What if they find parts of me uneaten?

He imagined Keahi trying to identify him from a recovered foot, part of an arm, his left side without a head. *Would tattoos help?* The kids he had seen on the beach had a barbed wire motif around their wrists and ankles. *If I survive, I'm getting a tattoo! Something unique. Maybe a Hawaiian war club?*

He wondered whether they would go to the trouble of cremation if there were only a few parts of him remaining. Wouldn't it be a joke if his ashes didn't fill even one pepper shaker? He smiled and then chuckled, thinking about his conversation with Keahi at the cemetery. It was all so absurd, so humiliating, so unrelenting … all so laughable!

Would it help to pray? But then he hadn't decided if God existed or not.

And then Keahi surfaced next to him.

"Thank goodness!" Liko exclaimed. "I thought I was shark bait!"

"We might still be," Keahi replied. "We've got an impossible swim ahead of us."

Keahi found it incredulous that Liko was in good humor. *What's wrong with the boy?* he wondered.

"How did you find me?"

"I figured that the current had taken you. So I let the current take me, too. Even swam with it to catch up. Then I heard you yelling. Then I saw your flashlight. We shouldn't talk, though. We'll need all our strength for the swim back."

Keahi didn't tell Liko, but when he had let the current sweep him out to sea, it had scared the hell out of him!

"I'm bleeding."

"What happened?"

"The coral. I lacerated my knee."

Then we ARE shark bait, Keahi thought, but he didn't tell Liko that either. "How bad?"

"I gouged it on the coral."

"You'll need tetanus and antibiotics." *If we survive.*

Keahi started swimming, pulling Liko along like a deflated raft. Although Liko didn't know it, Keahi swam parallel to the shore for a long, long time. He was deliberately swimming crosscurrent. Then Keahi changed directions and kicked diagonally back towards the shore, perhaps on an intercept course with the dive boat, perhaps not. Liko tried to kick too, but with little effect. He was cold and exhausted.

They were both silent.

Keahi expected a shark to strike his feet at any moment. It was Liko who was bleeding, but it was his feet that were scissoring through the water.

When they finally saw the boat's light again, and the boat grew on the horizon—first to the size of Keahi's thumb, then the size of his hand—only then did Keahi believe that they might make it. And when they reached the boat, silent tears ran down his cheeks and mixed with the salt water on his face. He was exhausted and had to be lifted aboard by three of the four other divers. An instructor helped Liko aboard.

To Liko's dismay, everyone sat watching them as the divemaster scolded them for becoming separated from the group.

"Another minute and I would have called the Coast Guard," the divemaster admonished. Liko detected a combination of fear and relief in the divemaster's voice.

Yeah, Keahi thought, *there is an Air Station at Kalaeloa. The Coast Guard would have scrambled a helicopter rescue team.*

Just more embarrassment, Liko thought.

Keahi was silent, and Liko was unable to look anyone in the eyes. Neither of them talked. They just sat across from each other shivering. A visitor loaned Liko an old red sweatshirt that said SUGAR BOWL 2008 and helped him pull it on. Another tourist shared his long sleeve shirt with Keahi, but it was too small. Keahi thanked him for the offer. The ride back to shore was cold and windy.

Blood ran down Liko's lower leg and slowly pooled at his foot. No one seemed to notice.

Sitting across from Liko, Keahi stared at the life-size bulldog's head on Liko's T-shirt. What a lopsided blowout that bowl game had been, Georgia Bulldogs 41, Hawaii Warriors 10: eight sacks, two fumbles, three interceptions, eleven penalties. During their first possession the Bulldogs had waltzed seventeen yards into the end zone, untouched. Keahi shook his head. Liko had no idea what he was wearing. *He doesn't know anything about the islands: his heritage, the local culture, and certainly not the ocean. And not even football!*

Liko saw Keahi frown, avert his eyes, and unconsciously shake his head with disappointment. *I've failed*, Liko thought. He was exhausted.

Liko, dejected, was people-watching at San Souci Beach on the Diamond Head side of the dilapidated natatorium. A short rock wall separated him from the white sandy beach and the sunbathers, swimmers and lifeguard. He shifted himself on the plastic park bench beneath the palm tree, resting the heels of his feet on the rock wall. He wasn't sure how long he had been sitting on the hard bench, but his butt was sore.

Three local kids swam in from the reef, carrying spear guns and snares for killing fish, octopus and eel. Keahi had told Liko that in the odd-numbered years, the reef in front of San Souci was open for fishing. These kids seemed intent on picking it clean. Liko watched them wash their masks and fins and other gear, and then shower near the steps leading down to the beach.

Since his Warrior Gym sunglasses had been stolen, Liko stayed close to San Souci and avoided the jetty where the local kids usually hung out and rode their boogie boards. He left them alone and they left him alone. Occasionally they would visit San Souci, or he would see signs that they had been there—cups and food wrappers discarded, or cigarette butts half-buried in the sand.

Now he watched the three kids gather their dead fish and limp octopus. He tracked them as they walked away in the direction of the jetty.

And then a young woman stepped into the shower and wet her long black hair and then her petite body. Her two-piece swimsuit changed from a light lilac to a dark mauve.

She stepped out of the cold shower. The water formed small beads among the goose bumps that had risen on her oiled shoulders, her flat stomach, her thighs. When she walked towards the ocean, the small beads flowed together, forming drops of water that fell from her body like diamonds in sunlight.

Liko watched her wade gracefully into the ocean. He watched her swim to the old windsock that was placed in the channel years earlier. She swam back. The water sparkled around her like silver confetti catching sunlight. He watched her wade out of the water and walk across the white sand to the shower, gracefully.

He noticed her feet; she had a slipper tan: a white, upside down V on both of her small feet.

She washed the sea salt from her long hair and olive tanned body and, to his amazement, she walked over to him, sat down and asked "Liko?"

"Yes?"

"I'm Toi. It's a beautiful day at the beach, isn't it?"

"Yes it is," he managed to say, flabbergasted. Then after a little hesitation, "Uh, I'm sorry, but how do you know my name?

"I work with your uncle."

"Oh."

"He told me that you liked to come here," Toi explained. "And it was easy to recognize you. You guys look alike, you and your uncle."

"I see." Liko nodded his head.

"He told me about Angelica and what happened at Hanauma Bay."

"Oh!" Liko groaned, suddenly discomfited.

"He also told me that you were swept away by the current. During your night dive, right?"

"Yes," Liko replied, now embarrassed.

"You're lucky to be alive."

"Why's that?"

"Because you don't know how to swim!"

She was a stranger admonishing him, yet, despite his embarrassment, instead of being offended he felt relieved. And that surprised him. "That's true," he confessed. "I can barely dogpaddle, much less swim."

"Well, you must learn!"

"I will," he said, suddenly making himself a promise.

Then he attempted a joke: "I've already taught myself to float."

"Not funny," Toi countered, shaking her head yet unable to hide a smile.

Then she looked right at him, "The ocean is unforgiving."

He nodded. "Well, it doesn't matter now anyway."

"Why not?"

"Because I'm going back to the States."

"Mainland," she corrected.

He read the expression on her face: she was surprised that he was leaving before the summer ended.

"It's too crowded in the studio," he explained. Actually, after the near-disastrous night dive, there just wasn't enough room in the studio to hold both Liko's humiliation and Keahi's disappointment.

"I hope I haven't upset you," Toi said. "I'm not usually this direct, but I can't sit back and let something terrible happen."

Liko looked closely at her face and her dark brown, slanted eyes. He knew that she was telling him the truth.

She is beautiful.

"Will you stay and watch the sunset with me?" he asked.

"Yes, I'd like that."

After the sunset, Liko gave her his phone number and e-mail in Nevada. That was a first for him.

The following Sunday afternoon, Liko, Keahi, Angelica and Carol were riding the waves in a rented outrigger canoe in front of the Ala Moana Surfrider Hotel. Carol was in the bow and Keahi was in the stern, providing rudder control. Seated behind Angelica, Liko watched Carol and Angelica's powerful muscles pull the canoe onto the top of a passing wave, their muscles like iron. Angelica stroked her paddle through the water, tirelessly, keeping rhythm with Carol, who was setting everyone's rhythm by shouting a cadence.

They rode the face of a curling wave as it pushed the canoe towards shore. White foam and salt spray surrounded them.

As the energy in the wave dissipated, the canoe slowed, and Keahi turned them around and they paddled back out to sea. Again they waited until another large wave approached and then they paddled hard in unison to Carol's chanting and caught the wave and rode it back in to shore. And then they caught another wave and another and another.

They were paddling instead of diving, which had been the original plan. After being admonished by Toi—she had lectured Keahi as well as Liko—Keahi had cancelled their remaining advanced scuba diving classes: the navigation dive and the deep dive. Quickly realizing how humiliated Liko was over the business, Keahi had proposed the canoeing.

But instead of enjoying the ride, Liko felt that they were babysitting him—Angelica and Carol in the bow, Keahi in the stern, and Liko protected in the middle. *I'm being treated like a child,* he thought.

That evening they held a farewell dinner for him at the Hau Tree Lanai restaurant in the hotel adjacent to San Souci. Tired, the four of them relaxed in white, wrought iron chairs arranged around a small, square table that was draped with a pink linen tablecloth. The table was beneath the spreading branches of an ancient hau tree, and Liko sat with his back a foot from its massive trunk.

Small white lights sparkled inside clear plastic tubing, strung on the underside of the branches like pearls on a necklace.

The sparkling lights reminded Liko of Toi. He remembered the water sparkling around her like silver confetti catching sunlight.

"Nice effect," Keahi said. "Isn't it?"

Before anyone could answer, Carol commented on the approaching rain. A wall of low, gray clouds was blowing from the mountains towards the ocean and their table.

Keahi looked overhead at the massive layer of intertwined, horizontal, tangled branches, and the dense cap of large, heart-shaped leaves. "This tree will keep us dry," he predicted.

They watched the gray clouds approach and talked story until their waiter returned to take their orders. Keahi insisted that Liko try the chef's *prix fixe* special, the most expensive item on the menu. Liko did not refuse. He ordered the soft shell crab bruschetta and, for an entrée, he chose a filet mignon of beef a la Florentine.

He had never tasted a soft-shelled crab and, to his surprise, he enjoyed it. The small crab was deep-fried and crispy, served on toast, and covered with a yellow mango and red pepper sauce and green, pungent arugula.

He finished his filet mignon just as the gray clouds and misty rain reached the hau tree and their table. As he cut and chewed his tenderloin, Liko marveled at the baby blue ocean, the gray clouds and the setting sun.

Keahi was right. The hau tree was better than an umbrella.

As they dined, the sun set into a gray cloud that floated just above the horizon. And then the sun reappeared beneath the cloud, and set a second time, like hot butter flowing.

"Incredible," Liko commented, taking a sip of water.

For dessert, everyone nibbled on the tiramisu that came with Liko's dinner. They fought over the two blackberries, one raspberry, a slice of green kiwi fruit, and two pieces of tangerine—all of which decorated the rich dessert.

Liko was enjoying himself, and by the time the tiramisu disappeared, so had his melancholy spirit.

After dinner they went to Keahi's studio and sat together on his lanai. Angelica sipped Amaretto, and Carol, Keahi and Liko shared two bottles of red wine. Keahi played his nose flute.

After a while, Liko excused himself and made a trip to the restroom. As he was returning, the phone shrilled.

"Hello," he answered.

Keahi thought that it was a call for him, so he set down his flute and started to get up, but then he heard Liko say in a pleased and happy voice, "I'm so glad you called. You know I'm leaving tonight?" And then Liko dropped down on the couch. "Yes, on the red-eye flight. The taxi will be picking me up soon."

Keahi rejoined the women on the lanai. They could tell by the tone of Liko's voice—soft and filled with music—that he was talking to a girl. Keahi looked at Carol, who raised an eyebrow, amused.

The phone conversation continued for some minutes, and then Liko hung up and returned to his seat on the lanai, next to Angelica. Angelica placed her hand on his and asked, "Who's your girlfriend?"

Liko smiled at Angelica. She was beautiful, with her sun-bleached blonde hair and green eyes. "An older, mature lady." Liko chuckled, trying to be nonchalant. "To protect her reputation—and especially to protect her from you guys—it is best that I don't reveal her identity. It's a small island, don't ya know?"

They laughed.

Keahi wanted to ask about the girl too, but he felt awkward, having just eavesdropped, so he kept quiet. Instead, he volunteered to talk to Liko's mother about Liko visiting again next summer.

The invitation broadsided Liko and, without thinking, he replied, "I'd like that." He immediately regretted it.

"Good," Keahi said, "I'll look forward to your visit next year."

Then he reminded Liko to keep his grades up, and that his great-aunt's offer to put him through college would always be an option.

When it was time for goodbyes, Carol gave him a bear hug that almost broke him in half. Angelica was gentler. She kissed him on each cheek, and then whispered in his ear, "Be good."

"I will," Liko said. Her beauty left him breathless.

Minutes later, seated alone in a shuttle bus, on his way to the airport, Liko was thinking about Toi. *I'm leaving the island and Toi for the trailer park and my mom.* He shook his head. By the time that the bus reached the airport, he had made a decision: *I'm going to return. And I'll learn how to swim! No more dogpaddling!*

Keahi felt this to be the loneliest time of day; everyone in the condominium complex was asleep, and he was sitting alone on his lanai watching the night breeze move the palms that surrounded the swimming pool. The underwater lights cast a muted, diffused glow on the small blue tiles that lined the pool. He was alone and he knew how upsetting such moments could be.

He thought about Liko, who was now on the overnight flight to Nevada. Keahi already missed him.

He thought about Angelica and his great-aunt and what they had said about him making a good father. Now, reflecting back on his summer with Liko, Keahi doubted it. Still, he wished Liko had stayed. That surprised him because he hadn't really wanted Liko to visit in the first place.

And who was Liko's mysterious girlfriend?

He felt sorry for Liko; starting a long distance romance would surely end in disappointment.

Keahi gazed into the night sky and saw the stars twinkling like diamonds set in black velvet.

He imagined that Daniel appeared to him and sat down on the edge of the pool, dangling his feet into the cool water. The surface rippled. The palm fronds rustled and a breeze blew through Daniel's thick hair. The underwater lights highlighted his dark features: his prominent chin, the mischievous dimple in his right check, and the twinkle in his dark eyes.

Keahi sighed and began a conversation. "I miss you Daniel."

He cracked another beer, closed his eyes and tasted the rich brew. "Daniel, I propose a toast. To all the lucky fathers and their sons." He raised his beer towards the wet, bright stars.

"I saved his life, Daniel. I saved his life twice: once at Hanauma Bay, and the second time during the night dive. You'd think that that would have earned his trust."

Daniel replied, "That was a nice touch, slipping that barbecue book into his new suitcase."

"I thought you would like that."

Keahi reached into his shirt pocket and took out the vial of oil from the Arizona Memorial. He inverted the glass vial and watched the black oil flow. It reminded him of adding molasses to rye flour when he made pumpernickel bread. *I should bake some bread tomorrow*, he thought.

Tomorrow . . . . Tomorrow was Monday and work, yet another reason to feel empty. Tomorrow he was scheduled to meet the new Head of Department, who had questions about the explosions at the meth lab and the child care center.

Keahi thought about the picture of the swing set that Little Bill had taken. Little Bill did funny things. *Imagine collecting something like that. It's morbid.*

He still had another six-pack of Foster's in the refrigerator and he planned to drink them all before he went to bed.

ABOUT THE AUTHOR

Greg Olmsted is an environmental health specialist. He lived in Hawaii for sixteen years. Olmsted hopes to use the arts to increase public awareness of environmental and public health issues. He resides with his wife in Washington, DC.

www.ingramcontent.com/pod-product-compliance
Lightning Source LLC
Chambersburg PA
CBHW050331110726
47899CB00007B/2456